RAMROD VENGEANCE

Burt Howard wanted only one thing—revenge on the man who had shot and killed his young fiancée. His vengeance was going to be hot lead in the bodies of the killers. To get them he had to ramrod an outfit for a woman—the last thing he ever wanted to do. But the game was played for high stakes and Burt was willing to pay the price—no matter what it cost him . . .

Also available from Gunsmoke

RAMROD VENGEANCE

William Hopson

WESTERNS

A-1

First published 1949
by Phoenix Press

This hardback edition 1991
by Chivers Press
by arrangement with
Donald MacCampbell, Inc.

ISBN 0 7451 4504 3

British Library Cataloguing in Publication Data available

Printed and bound in Great Britain by
Redwood Press Limited, Melksham, Wiltshire

Chapter 1

IT HAD BEEN old Al Tracy, ex-Army scout and trapper and Indian fighter, who had sent him the word: a laboriously scrawled note, barely decipherable; a piece of paper from a wrapped package. But it gave Burt Howard the answer he'd been waiting more than two years to find.

Delgadito had finally been caught. He'd slipped across the border just once too often since the massacre of more than two years ago. He was in jail in Yuma, and Al's note had said that he would talk.

Howard came out of the desert wastes at sundown that day, from the direction of San Diego, where he'd received the letter. It had been a long, torturous ride over first the mountains and then across the desert, eastward toward the Colorado River and Yuma; pushing his two mounts to the limit, hoping to get there before they tried and hung the Apache.

He rode past the Yuma Indian Reservation, a gaunt, haggard man looking a little older than twenty-nine. Dogs barked at him and fat, sloe-eyed squaws looked curiously while the dogs barked again and the children hooted at him. He paid them no heed. His eyes were on the outlines of the fort yonder on the hill and, across the river, the grim walls and cells of the Yuma territorial prison.

He's in there, Howard thought. They wouldn't dare keep him any place else. Not Delgadito. He's in there and I'm going to meet him face to face.

He wondered what his emotions would be. She'd been

5

dead two and a half years now, she who had waited for him at the ranch that night, and he wondered what had been her last hours, her last minutes, about the fear that must have struck her as they took her out and clubbed or shot her or stabbed her throat.

Time had dulled the ache and the memories of her a little, and he didn't know whether or not he would hate the Apache with rising fury for what he had done.

If only he *knows*, Howard thought. If he can only tell me the name or give me the description of the man who plotted it.

Howard rode on, heading for the ferry. Whatever the answer, he would soon know. Then would begin the job that already had occupied him for so long: tracking down and killing the man who had caused Dora's death.

The sun was almost down when Howard rode his horse and led his lightly packed mount onto the floor of the ferry. The two Indians started across. From behind them, in the fort on the hill, a bugle blew and the flag at the top of the pole began its descent to the ground, limp in the breezeless air. The waters of the Colorado rolled and made sluggish little whirlpools on their way to Mexico twenty-six miles away and thence into the gulf. The prison loomed up closer as the ferry grounded bumpily. Burt Howard paid the two stolid Indians and led his horse up the banked road and then mounted. Half a mile away he saw the main street of Yuma.

He curbed his impatience now, for the job was almost done. It had been a hard, fast trip with impatience in every mile. Now there seemed to be a world of time. He looked up at the cell doors back of which men were locked under four feet of solid stone; cells with big iron rings sunk in the concrete floors, to hold the chains of the Indians, Mexicans, Negroes, and the whites who shared their lives. The worst desperadoes in Arizona Territory. Howard rode on and came to a livery. He left his two horses to be cared for and went over to a hotel. The hotel looked like about the only

6

building in town that wasn't adobe. It was operated by the railroad.

"How long will you be with us, sir?" the clerk asked. "Just for tonight, or will it be longer?"

"That, friend, is something that I do not know," Howard said softly. "Know where I can find a man named Al Tracy?"

"That crippled up old Indian fighter? Sure, any place up and down Main Street where there's a domino or checker game. Try the saloons. Don't know where he lives."

Howard said a brief, "Thanks," and took the key upstairs. He threw his saddle bags on the bed and unbuckled his gunbelt, tossing it by the bags. It wasn't until after he had scraped away a five-day growth of brown-reddish pig bristles and sand that he saw how gaunt his face had become. It was the result of the ride, the new fire which had burned within him since he had received Al's letter. There were new lines in his face, around the light-colored eyes. His eyebrows were inclined to be a trifle heavy, though not shaggy. His nose curved downward in a thin ridge to the tip. The mouth was expressionless.

"Anyhow, I'll know pretty soon now, maybe tonight," he said, and then the fire and the impatience were suddenly flaming inside him again. They came up like a rising surge of water in a stream as narrow as his body.

He put on his shirt and went down to the dining room. He had to eat first, after days on the trail with meals of his own scanty fare. He had ridden all day except for two hours at noon to escape the heat that almost put the horses down. He was hungry.

That done, he lit a cigarette and strolled out on the porch and down the flight of six steps to the ground. Main Street was quiet, the heat that had poured down upon it all day and had been reflected from the buildings seemingly reluctant to depart. It had soaked in and wouldn't leave until after midnight.

Howard looked in on several saloons and pool halls. A

7

little Mexican boy came up and said, "Shine, Meester? Two penny an' I geeve you wan gude shine."

"All right," Howard said, and leaned back against a wall, lifting a boot.

But Tracy didn't come along, and afterward he went on. He guessed that perhaps the old man might be home.

He was, but an hour later Burt Howard found him getting ready to sit down to a game of checkers. He caught the bearded old man's eye and inclined his head in a brief nod. Al limpingly followed him out into the street, using a cane. An Apache had ambushed him fifteen years before while he was on a mission for the Army and crippled him for life, though he could still ride. A broken down old man of eighty who had first come to Yuma in 1836.

Howard waited, and again there was the new, sudden fear that he might be too late; that Delgadito the Apache raider might already have been hung for any of a dozen murderous crimes.

"You git my letter I writ?" Al demanded, shaking hands.

Howard nodded. "Am I too late?"

Al's dirty beard wagged sideways. He had once had a Yuma squaw, but she had died a few years previously.

"Where is he?" Howard asked.

Al half turned and pointed with his cane in the direction of the fortress-like walls over on the hill. "They got him in a special cell all by hisself with a handcuff on one wrist and a leg iron on one leg. Both them irons are attached to two chains runnin' from wrist an' ankle to a ring in the floor."

"Have you talked to him?"

"Sure. Told the warden he was an old friend of mine, ha, ha! I ast him about the massacree at the Henderson ranch that night. He remembers the girl all right. He wore her ring in an ear for a while. Ain't no use for me to tell you what happened to her or how they killed her. 'Twon't do no good nohow."

"No," Burt Howard said, "it would do no good. I got there

8

the day after the funeral. What did he say about another man—a white man connected with it?"

"He says he wants money for a lawyer—though little good that'll do 'im, I can tell you. Three hundred dollars. You got it?"

"Yes," Howard said.

"Then let's git a rig and go see him. I ain't promisin' you nothin', Burt. But I told him he musta been tipped off on the gold that stage was carrying when your girl was comin' west to marry you. I ast him how come when the stage stopped at the ranch fer a change of hosses, he and them other bucks in the band was waitin'? How come they didn't hit the stage from ambush? I ast him how come there happened to be four boxes of new rifles an' ammernition on the stage him an' his bucks ambushed there in the ranch yard that night? So he said he'd see you for three hundred."

It was dark when they drove up the hill in an open-topped buggy drawn by a flea-bitten roan horse, and pulled up by the entrance. Howard tied the pony to a hitch rack as Al got gruntingly out.

Much of it was coming back now. There was the pain of remembering how he'd met Dora while on a trip back East. There had been months of waiting until she had come to him, to take up life on a prosperous desert ranch Howard owned. At an Army post town, four crates of rifles from the arsenal had been loaded and lashed atop the stage for delivery to a small fort two hundred miles away. And on the following day eighty thousand dollars in gold had been put on at a town called Hatrack. She had been on that stage when it had rolled into the ranch yard for a quick change of horses and a bite to eat for the passengers. And Dora had been the only one.

It was then that the raiders under Delgadito had struck. They had shot the guard and stage driver first, then swarmed into the house and killed Henderson, his wife, and two small sons. And they had killed, Dora too, while the others

9

murdered two riders and several Mexican field hands. A massacre.

That was near as men had been able to piece together the story. Burt Howard hadn't received the news until the next stage brought it. He had waited for the first, which never arrived. He had saddled and gone back, but by then it was too late. She had been buried one day when he got there.

The rifles were gone, the gold gone; vanished into the desert wastes, heading south at a hard clip for sanctuary across the Mexican border. But there had been something about it that hadn't clicked right in Burt Howard's mind for a long time afterward. She was dead and couldn't be brought back; the law officers and the soldiers had read it as an attack which happened to bag a rich prize. But something told Howard that it might not be a coincidence. And the hardcase in him said that he'd never rest until he found out.

He's started in Hatrack on a patient job of finding out who knew about the gold and the guns coming through. It had gone on for months while he worked all the way back to the command post from which the rifles had been shipped. But the trail always led back to Hatrack and Wells-Fargo, where the Old Woman Mine payroll had been loaded. It had centered on a man named Broadhurst. But he could learn no trace of the man's background, how he might have gotten in touch with Delgadito, or where he had disappeared to a month after the massacre.

So it had been a matter of selling his ranch and beginning the hunt for the man who answered Broadhurst's description; leaving word with men like Al Tracy—and waiting for the day when Delgadito might be captured.

And now they had him.

Chapter 2

THERE WAS a guard room beside the entrance and they went in. Al Tracy said, "Howdy, Leon," to the head night guard, an angular, bony-faced man with a sagging blond mustache.

"Howdy, Al. Howdy, Mister," to Burt.

Burt shook hands briefly at Tracy's introduction. "Leon, we went to see Delgadito," the old scout said.

Leon shook his head. "Sorry, old-timer. No can do. Warden's orders. Nobody can look in on him except the guard in front of his cell."

"We don't want to look in at him. We want to go inside and talk with him. Privately," Burt Howard murmured.

"Couldn't think of it, boys. Out of the question."

"Leon, do you remember the Henderson ranch massacre two years or so ago?" Al Tracy asked. "And that girl who was clubbed—was killed?"

"Be a long time before I forget, with me holding the dirty dog that did it," grunted the head night guard.

"Well, Burt don't like to talk about it any more, but that Eastern girl who was on that stage was comin' to marry him. She never got there on account of Burt thinks there was some dog of a white man who tipped them off about those guns and that gold. Burt don't give a hoot or a holler about the guns or gold. He just wants to find that white man. Now look here, Leon: the warden has let me in to see him several times and he shore wouldn't object if he knew what we wanted. We only need a few minutes."

The guard looked questioningly at Burt, saw the

bitterness and suffering in the drawn face. He got up and took a big key ring from a drawer of the desk.

"Come with me," he said. "I've got a wife myself, Howard."

He unlocked two iron gates, passed into a tunnel made of 'dobie bricks to a depth and thickness of six feet, and locked the gates once more.

They came out into a lighted place where a guard sat in a chair with his back to the adobe wall in such a manner he could survey the space between two rows of cells. The cells had roofs of solid rock nearly five feet in thickness. They walked the length of the cells, hearing the murmur of voices, the rattle of a chain, the snores of those dog tired from twelve hours at hard labor in the terrible heat and sun. Yuma housed the toughest men in the territory, but none was too tough for the prison. It was a place where men worked in one hundred and ten degrees of heat in the shade, where the whipping post helped tame them all, a place where where too often, when a man didn't answer roll call, they went into his cell and carried him out and down below the hill to a rocky promontory by the Colorado River. There they buried him in rock and branded his name on a plan board and forgot that he had ever existed.

The three men came to another iron gate, which the head night guard unlocked, and then locked behind them. This time the line of cells were mere caves with doors in what looked like a wall of solid rock thirty feet high and forty long. These cells formed a "T" with the others. There was a small courtyard in between the two.

A lantern hung from a pole, and beneath it a guard sat in a chair and slapped at the insects buzzing around the light. He got up and said, "What's old Al done now, Leon? Where'll we put him—in one of the end dungeons?"

Howard didn't hear the answer. Leon had already pointed to a door to one of the dungeons. He said, "He's in there with one chain on his wrist and another on his leg, and both

12

padlocked to a ring in the floor until the Army and the civil authorities settle their fight to see who hangs him." And Burt Howard had the slightly incredulous feeling that, after two and a half years, he was finally going to meet the man.

"I'd better go on in first, Burt," Al Tracy said. "Sort of prepare him for you. I'll tell him you got the three hundred."

"All right," Howard said.

"You're not packing a gun, are you?" the head guard asked sharply.

"No," answered Burt.

"Raise your hands."

Burt Howard raised them. The guard patted him over for a short gun, went on down his trouser legs to his boot tops and felt around in them for a knife or pistol hideout.

"Got a knife?"

Burt handed over his jackknife. "I hold no personal grudge against the man," he said. "He massacred people he considered his enemies. I just want to find out if he did it on his own or if somebody plotted it for him."

"I understand. If there was, then he, not the Indian, was really responsible for the death of your sweetheart. All right, you'll soon know."

He went over and took another lantern off another pole and walked over to the door of the dungeon. It was solid iron except for a small door that could be opened. The guard opened it and peered in between the bars, holding his lantern high. Howard heard the rattle of a chain. The guard unlocked the door and looked inside. Then he stepped back and handed the lantern to Al Tracy. He nodded. Howard stood back beside the guard.

"He's a mean devil," Burt said absently. He could hear low gutturals from within.

"They all are," Leon said. "Two weeks ago a couple of deputy sheriffs started for here in a light wagon with four of them in handcuffs and chained. They never showed up. Day before yesterday a rancher over east of here found what was left of them. It wasn't much, after the coyotes and buzzards and hot sun got through with them. Nobody knows what happened, but the red devils got the advantage of them somehow, killed them, and took off with the wagon and team. There's Al. I guess you can go in."

Burt stepped in, bending to enter through the low doorway. He found himself in a surprisingly cool dungeon with walls and ceiling of solid rock and mortar. An offensive smell, the smell of an unwashed human body and of human offal, hit his nostrils; the kind of a smell one might find in the lair of a wild animal. A chain rattled, and in the dim light of the smoky lantern sitting on the floor Burt saw first a pair of naked feet, almost black, with a chain leading from one to a ring in the center of the floor. He saw dirty pants without a belt, a rag of a shirt, a face almost as black as that of a Negro.

A thin face with evil written all over it, and black hair cut short enough so that it couldn't be tied around the throat and used to strangle himself. Delgadito sat on a filthy mattress on the rock floor. His eyes met those of Burt Howard. They were opaque, without emotion.

"He wants to tell you all about what happened at the ranch that night," Al Tracy said. "They like to talk about those things, particularly since he ain't had a chance to powwow in his own lingo fer a couple of weeks and he only knows about a dozen words of Spanish."

"It's all done . . . finished," Burt Howard said in a voice devoid of all tone. "Ask him if he knew before that attack in the ranch yard that night that the stage had guns and gold."

The aged old scout was half sitting, half squatting on the floor. He couldn't sit cross-legged because of his bad leg. He spoke gutturally and his hands made many motions. Delgadito's wrist chain rattled as he answered back both by sign and by voice.

"He wants to see the color of your money first," Al interpreted.

Howard reached into his pocket and brought out fifteen

14

gold double-eagles. He gave them to the scout. Delgadito began to talk. Al nodded and listened. It took five minutes before he could get in what appeared to be a question, and Howard realized that Delgadito was relating the account of the fight, and probably boasting as such men liked to do.

Al nodded again and looked up. "He'll have to tell the whole story again, but it's coming through."

The Apache sitting in chains on the mattress asked a question. Al Tracy said, "He wants to know if you'd like to find out how they killed the girl. He thinks it's her you want to know about."

"No," Burt Howard answered harshly. "I just want the name and description of the man who plotted that murderous business."

Delgadito began to talk again, the chain on his left wrist rattling as he made signs. Finally it was over.

Al twisted his bad leg to ease the circulation and looked up once more.

"Here's about the way it runs," he said. "He was in Hatrack one day from the reservation and met a man who spoke his own tongue. He—"

"What kind of a man?" snapped Burt.

"Now, look here, he told it *his* way, so you lemme tell it *my* way!" protested the old man. "He says as how he met this feller, and because he was a white man who spoke the Apache lingo he figgered him to be a friend of the Indians. He'd talk to him ever' time he come to town. Finally this feller tells him that in about three weeks there is going to be much gold on the stage. The white soldiers also had sent a message that on about the same date they were shipping many new rifles and shells to another fort. If he and his men would break off the reservation and take the stage, there would be many new rifles and ammunition. Delgadito says as how the white men had taken all the guns away from his people and he wanted some new ones so's he could go on into Mexico and join the Sonora Apaches down there and be free

15

again to fight the white man. So they high-tailed it off the reservation on the night agreed upon, and this feller was waiting for them out of town at a place that had been set. He told 'em the stage would stop at this ranch at sundown the next day with the gold and guns and for them to take it there, take the guns for themsleves, and bury the gold for him under the harness shed and then burn it down. So that's what they did. He said he didn't want the white man's gold because it was no good to a great warrior living in Sonora. Well, they hit the place, killed everybody on the ranch, burned the barn, and lit a shuck for the border with the new guns. He said they tried to burn the ranch too, but it was adobe and didn't burn on the inside, 'cept for the floors and the furniture. That's all he knows."

"What did the man look like?"

After more talk in Apache, Al said, "Big man. Big arms. Big shoulders. That's about all he can describe."

"Where did he work?"

That one brought a shrug. "He don't know," from Al. "Said he always met the man some place where he could slip him a pint of whiskey."

Leon, the head night guard, stuck his head in through the door. "Hurry it up, boys. The warden sometimes rides up nights to look things over. I'd druther he don't find you here with this cell door unlocked. I might catch the devil."

They talked a bit more and left. Outside, in front of the guard office, Leon turned.

"I heard some of it. I hope you find him."

Howard said, "Thanks," and drove back to town, not paying much attention to Al's garrulous talk. The old man was quite proud of the job he had done.

"Ain't talked thet lingo in nearly ten year but I can still cut 'er," he said happily. "I wish it war twenty year back an' I was out chasin' the red devils ag'in."

Burt didn't answer; his mind was on other things. A big man who spoke the Apache language. Delgadito hadn't

16

known his name, where he worked.

At any rate, it was a lead now. A definite lead. He had to find that man.

He sold his horses the next morning and returned by stage to Hatrack and went straight to the Army post not far from the reservation and asked if they had ever employed a big man who spoke Apache as a scout, interpreter or guide. The answer was a shake of the head. Burt returned to town and wrote a letter to the Army in Washington, posing the same question. He waited three months for an answer that never came. The letter either had been snarled up in office routine or ignored as the work of a crank. He didn't even know the man's name. Meanwhile, during those three months he covered every Army post in Arizona territory, and by fall he knew that his work had been fruitless. The man who had plotted the massacre had not learned Apache in Arizona.

So as the weather began to turn colder Burt Howard drew the proceeds from the sale of his ranch and took the stage east, into the Mescalero Apache country of New Mexico. Again it was one fort after another, with the same answer, until there came a day when he rode into an outpost in the Indian country. It was the same routine of asking permission to see the commanding officer, waiting for the orderly to return and nod for him to go in, asking the same question he'd asked so many times before.

"I'm looking for a big man whose name I do not know. He's one of the few white men who speak Apache fluently. Have you ever employed such a man as scout or clerk or interpreter?"

The wiry little colonel back of the desk answered instantly, "Big fellow, you say? Sort of red-haired and strong as a bull? That sounds like John Broadhurst to me. Yes, we had him here..."

Burt Howard didn't hear the rest of it. The name seemed to explode in his brain.

Broadhurst, the Wells-Fargo man!

17

Everything came clear in a flash. Broadhurst had kept his past a closely guarded secret, planned the massacre, waited a month, and then gone into the ruins of a now abandoned and burned out ranch and taken his buried gold from the grey ashes of the burned barn!

"When he applied for employment here," the officer was saying, "he gave the information that he had been raised among the Indians in this country and spoke their language as well as his own. We called in a couple of Apache police who not only talked with him but seemed to know him. So we hired him as a scout. But that's been all of three years ago. He drew his pay and disappeared. We haven't seen him since."

Howard thanked the colonel and went back to his hotel room. His months of painstaking man-tracking had finally brought results. He had identified his man.

He lay there in the bed that night and thought out his next move. Where would Broadhurst be now?

He had been raised in the Southwest. He might have taken an Eastern fling with his eighty thousand dollars, but the East would not be for him. He would come back to the Southwest, somewhere. He had been a scout, which meant that he was a rider who undoubtedly knew cattle; and the railroads in Kansas were making the trail drivers rich as they pushed the big herds of longhorns up the trail...

Burt jumped out of bed and fumbled for a match. He lit the lamp and began to write letters feverishly. One to Arizona, one to Santa Fe in New Mexico, and one to Austin, Texas. Nearly a month went by and the first snows came before he began to receive replies.

Yes, the letter from Austin said, there was a John Broadhurst who had a JB iron registered from Carterville, Texas.

Burt Howard sat there in the hotel room and lit a match to the letter and watched it burn until he had to drop the last corner.

18

He had found his man.

For three years he had engaged in a search that had become almost an obsession with him.

And now the search was ended.

Chapter 3

THE AFTERNOON stage came into Carterville about five that day, trying to outrun a norther that was sweeping down across the plains. The wind whipped at the trees and struck at the foothills, whistling up the gullies as though in search of the cattle already seeking shelter. It was, as the driver had said, "goin' to be a hummer."

Inside the stage, Burt Howard sat beside a pretty young woman of about twenty-four, who held a bundled up baby on her lap. Although the canvas covers had been drawn, it was bitterly cold inside the stage. Howard's booted feet felt like ice. It had been a five-hour trip and the child, a girl of about four, had been fretful. Howard had taken turns holding her to relieve the tired mother. Her name, she had said, was Mrs. Clay and they were coming to Carterville to live with relatives. Her husband was dead.

When the stage rolled up in front of the Wells-Fargo building on a corner, Howard got down stiffly, his joints creaking from the cold. He held out his arms for the child and waited while one of the two other men passengers assisted the mother to alight. They went inside to warm themselves at a big fat stove while the driver brought in the mail sacks and a hostler took care of baggage.

Burt put down the child and removed her heavy wrap. They all stood by the stove warming themselves. Over on a bench three men lounged and looked at the newcomers. At the feet of one of them lay a massive brown mastiff, head pillowed on its forepaws. Howard unbuttoned his mackinaw as the heat began to soak into his chilled body.

"I guess the folks didn't think we'd be in," Mrs. Clay said a little nervously. "I don't know where they live."

"I expect there are hacks for hire at the livery," Howard said. "You won't have to walk."

He looked down at the child, thinking that if it hadn't been for a man named John Broadhurst, he might have had one like her. She had toddled over and laid her hand on the huge mastiff's head.

What happened then was like a nightmare lasting a few split seconds; it froze Burt's blood. The mastiff let out a savage snarl and swung gaping jaws at the girl. Only the fact that she stood against him saved her from the flaming-eyed animal. It swung with gaping jaws wide and knocked her backward. As she fell it came up on big legs and leaped, jaws wide open.

Then it seemed to pause in mid-air as the crash of an exploding .45 almost deafened the room's occupants. The six-shooter roared again and the mastiff was down.

Burt sheathed the heavy six-shooter and bent, pushing the dog's carcass off the child it had tried to kill. He picked up the crying girl and handed her to her mother.

"I don't think she's hurt, just badly scared—and I don't blame her," he said.

He turned. The man who had sat in the middle on the bench had come to his feet. He was thirty, powerfully built, with a pair of hard, piercing blue eyes that looked into Howard's.

"I'm plumb sorry if your little girl fooled with Rex, mister, but people hadn't ought to let their kids monkey with strange dogs."

"People with dogs like that one shouldn't have them around where babies can monkey with them," Burt Howard said. "And I'm not the child's father. She hasn't got one."

"Stranger, eh? Where from?"

21

"That's my business," was the clipped reply.

"John Broadhurst might make it his. He was plenty fond of that dog."

"Mrs. Clay is plenty fond of her child. I expect that John Broadhurst will have to find himself another pet."

The other two men had come up and were standing warily, stiffly.

"What's your name?" the big man asked. "John might want to know."

Burt said, "Then let John come ask me."

"Hardcase, eh?" sneered the other.

"Look, mister," Burt Howard said evenly. "You've said enough. Now you either put up or shut up. I shot that brute. And if you think enough of this John Broadhurst to do something about it, then start doing it."

His hand lay close by his hip, the mackinaw shoved back. There were still three cartridges left in the .45, for Burt seldom carried a live round beneath the hammer.

The bigger man said, "Come on," and led the way to the door, followed by the others. The driver stood in the open doorway, mail sacks over one shoulder and a package under one arm. Over his shoulder peered the face of the hostler. They gave way and the three men disappeared into the wind of the street.

The driver kicked the door shut with one foot and strode over to the counter where he dumped the sacks and package. He turned. Nobody had spoken in the strained silence. He saw the bloody carcass of the once vicious mastiff on the floor.

"That's Broadhurst's dog, ain't it? What happened?" he asked.

"It *was* John's dog," the clerk put in a correction. "What happened was that the tyke toddled over to touch it and Rex tried to tear it to pieces. It'd a done so too, except that this stranger here blasted it with a forty-five. It was at the tyke's throat when the first one caught it and knocked it back. The

22

second one sure made a mess of its head. Some mess for me to clean up," he added.

The driver had a broken nose, slightly crooked, and a scar through one eyebrow, probably mementoes of a brawl in which beer bottles had been used in lieu of fists. He looked at Burt.

"I didn't get your name on the way down," he said.

"Burt Howard," was the reply. "My bags down yet?"

"They'll be in in a minute. Look, Howard, I don't like to see strangers get in trouble in Carterville. That big gent you were jawin' with over the dog is Buck Lake, Broadhurst's ranch foreman. He's foreman not because he's a better cowhand than some of the others but because he's tougher. He's a mean man who don't forget. You backed him down and he won't forget *that* either. If you're travelin' through, get a room at one of the small hotels—not Broadhurst's— and keep outa sight until morn'. There's a small bridge crosses the crick a half-mile below town, and I'll be by there at eight-thirty. I'll pick you up there."

"Thanks, but I kind of figured I'll stick around for a while,"

The driver shrugged. "It's your funeral, mister." He turned to the clerk. "Lordy, what a trip! Coldest run I ever made, an' I been drivin' thet stage a long time."

Mrs. Clay came over. The child had stopped crying now. The woman said, timidly and low-voiced, "I'm sorry about what happened, Mr. Howard. But I'm very grateful too. If there's anything that my family and I can do for you, just let us know."

"Thanks," he answered. "You wait here and I'll see if I can find you a rig."

He asked the clerk, nodded, and went out into the bite of the wind that was causing little dust devils to swirl along the street. Horses stood humped at hitch racks, hips slumped against the wind, eyes shut to keep out the dust. Down the street a way Howard saw a two-story building with an upper

23

and lower veranda, enclosed by railings. The sign said, *Broadhurst Hotel*, and Howard thought fleetingly: He's done all right with the eighty thousand he got from the massacre. An iron and a hotel...and a bad dog to follow a bad foreman around.

He pulled his hat down a bit more against the wind and went toward the livery. He came back an hour later, riding beside a stablehand. He helped load the woman's baggage, lifted up the child to her lap, and went back with her thanks following him, closing the door of the office behind him.

His baggage was piled on the floor, waiting for him. One of the canvas sacks contained his saddle, bridle, rope and spurs. The other was a tightly laced warbag from which protruded the worn stock of a rifle. It was a gun of heavy caliber and long range; a gun for Apache country. Howard picked up two small bags.

"I'd like to leave the others here for a bit," he said.

"Sure, sure, anything to oblige," the clerk agreed. "I'll put 'em back here in the corner behind the counter. You can call for 'em any time. We're open from eight in the mornin' until six. Glad to oblige."

Howard again went out into the wind, which was getting colder. He made his way down the street and went up the steps to the veranda of the Broadhurst Hotel. There might be a dozen other John Broadhursts besides this one. He shifted the two bags to one hand and opened the door and went in.

There was a big stove in one corner of the lobby, a monster affair. Back of it was a large stack of dry mesquite wood, cut in three-foot lengths. A dozen or so people, refugees from the biting wind outside, lounged in the lobby. Conversation dropped to a minimum as he entered, and Burt knew that word of the incident had gone like a flash through the town. He saw the man Buck Lake and he saw the two others with him. He went over to the counter and put down the bags.

"Got one?" he asked of the clerk.

"Yes, sir. First or second floor?"

"Second. And on the south side, away from the wind."

He signed the register and reached to pick up his bags. He straightened and turned and looked at Lake and the two others, who had converged. Nine other men sat watching; cowmen and nesters and town loafers. Under an arch leading past the end of the counter into the dining room, a waitress had paused with a cup of steaming coffee in one hand.

"I thought," Burt Howard said, "that we settled it up there at the stage station a little while ago."

"Here comes John," Buck Lake said.

Broadhurst came in from the dining room. A big man, the little colonel over at the fort in New Mexico had said. Sandy-haired. A big man, Delgadito had said. Big arms, big shoulders. Burt saw the golden hair on the back of the man's hands, the sandy hair above a pair of half quizzical, half amused eyes.

It was *the* John Broadhurst, all right.

This was late January. It had happened in April. Three years next April. And now he had tracked down and come face to face with the man from whom he was going to exact the price of a massacre.

Chapter 4

BROADHURST MOVED in closer, a napkin in one hand. He apparently had left a dining table. He rolled a toothpick in his mouth.

"So you're this Howard fellow?" he asked.

"I'm the man who shot your dog," Burt said.

"Oh, yes. Too bad about that. Rex wasn't used to children."

"So I noticed. Anything else on your mind?"

Broadhurst murmured the same word Buck Lake had said up in the Wells-Fargo station, "Hardcase," and then went on, "We'll forget about the dog. Very regrettable incident. Anything between you and Buck is, of course, none of my affair. He's a little sensitive about some things."

So that was it? It was an invitation to Lake to square up for the incident up the street.

"Anything else?" Howard asked.

"Looking for a job?"

"I'm in no hurry."

"Too cold, eh, when you have a few dollars to loaf where it's warm? But the offer is open. We'll have a spring roundup on one of these days, and Buck can use good men."

That was an invitation, too. To get him on the ranch where Buck Lake could square accounts.

"Not interested," Burt said curtly, and bent to pick up his bags.

"In that case," Buck Lake's voice said, "I might as well square up now."

He was unbuckling his gunbelt, and a tension that was electric went through the room. Burt straightened again.

"Some other time," he said curtly.

Broadhurst said to one of the men who was with Lake, a dark-faced rider, "Take the man's gunbelt and hold it for him, Kansas. I really did think a lot of Rex."

Howard saw the extended hand of the rider. He slid out of his mackinaw and laid it on the counter. He unbuckled his gunbelt and half turned to put it on top of the coat when the smashing blow came. Lake hadn't struck at his jaw. He had struck at his stomach; to knock the wind out of him, to paralyze him to leave him weak and gasping, ready to be finished off.

The blow landed squarely. It struck the thick leather money belt in which reposed nearly twenty thousand dollars in gold notes; the proceeds from the sale of the ranch three years before. It drove Howard back along the counter just far enough so that he had time to regain his balance.

Then he dived for the bigger man. He caught him head first in the belly and the wind went out of Lake as he went down. Burt was on him in a flash, but not to hit. He stepped on a booted ankle and pinned it to the floor. He grabbed the other ankle and lifted it and twisted cruelly on the boot. He stood with legs braced and Lake lay with his legs in a "V" with the bones creaking, and a strangled bawl of pain came from him.

Howard continued the pressure, knowing what those split legs were doing to the thigh bones. He twisted the boot harder and another gasping groan of pain burst from Lake's twisted lips.

From somewhere behind Burt, in the arch leading to the kitchen, came laughter; a woman's laughter that was musical and rich and gay. He turned and saw her, a woman of about twenty-five or so in boots and a riding skirt and a white blouse, with a mass of brown hair coiled high above her very pretty face.

27

"Oh, John, this is rich!" she half shrieked, and went off into further peals of laughter. "So Buck was going to beat him up like he's beaten up so many other men, and you were going to enjoy it because he killed that brute of a vicious dog? Twist it, cowboy! Break it!"

Movement came from behind and the muzzle of Kansas' gun jabbed Howard in the back. He let go and turned slowly. Lake got up, grunting, his face a mask of murderous hate. He limped and then crouched.

"I'm going to break you apart, mister," came his voice.

Another voice, softer, said, "No, you're not, Buck. Drop that gun, Kansas, or I'll shoot your entrails out."

She had jumped in behind the counter. She leaned over it, Burt's .45 leveled at the two men. "You dogs," she said levelly. "You cowardly cur dogs. No wonder Rex liked you so much, Buck. The two of you must have come from the same litter."

Kansas slid his gun back into its sheath beneath his coat. Lake had straightened, no more fight in him for the time being. He was panting a little but he made no move.

"Come over and get your gunbelt, cowboy," she said. "I'll see that the big bold Buck doesn't make another cowardly try while your back is turned. Here."

She held out the belt with its empty sheath. Howard began buckling it on and Broadhurst looked at Buck Lake.

He said, "You fight your own battles. This round is his. Maybe a ride back to the ranch in this wind will cool you off a bit. You and Kansas and Luke get going. Looks like the first round went to Howard."

Lake was slipping his own belt into place around his heavy waist. He looked at Burt Howard.

"Round one," he nodded, and went out.

Howard put on his mackinaw again and bent for his bags. The woman came over and stuck out her hand. Her eyes were appraising, and she apparently liked what she saw.

"You'll do. I'm Nell Corley."

28

"Glad to meet you, Miss Corley," he said, and let the hand drop. "I'm Burt Howard. Thanks for stepping in."

She laughed that laugh again. "My motives were purely selfish, Burt. I didn't want to see what looks like a first-class cowhand put out of commission because of a few stomped in ribs and a stomped in face. That's Buck's specialty with the men he whips . . . John's approval, of course," she added.

"Nell, some day you're going too far," Broadhurst warned her. "I can stand just so much, even from a woman."

She smiled at him, and then at Burt. "John is a very frustrated man, Burt. He came in here about two and a half years ago and bought the old Vinegarroon spread on Vinegarroon Creek. It's north of the holdings I inherited. He wanted to buy me out at first. When that wouldn't work he tried to *marry* the place. But that didn't work either. So now he's trying to drive me out. That's why I stepped in. Buck would have got you in time. He's too big and tough to be caught a second time. I figured you'd be of a lot more value working for me against his hardcase crew than a cripple for the rest of your life. Will you take the job?"

"Thanks, Miss Corley. Not interested."

"Mister," John Broadhurst put in quietly, "you've got more of a head on you than I thought."

He went back into the dining room and Howard ascended the stairs, key in hand.

The room was on the south side, away from the wind. It was icy cold inside, and Howard went to the small stove and looked in. Paper, kindling, and wood were waiting. He lit a match, put a pan of water on top of the stove, and began to unpack shaving outfit and a clean shirt. When the room was a little warmer he stripped off the old shirt and began to shave. He finished, dressed, and put on a brown corduroy coat, much lighter than the storm-proof mackinaw. By the time he descended the stairs again the dining room was less busy. Men in the lobby looked at him, but he ignored them and entered the dining room. Broadhurst was nowhere to be seen, but in a far corner Nell Corley was waiting.

She beckoned and he went over, threading his way among the tables.

"Sit down, Burt," she said. "I've drunk four cups of coffee waiting for you."

"If it's about the job, Nell, the answer is still the same."

"Why?" she asked.

He shrugged that one off and waited for the waitress to place a glass of water in front of him. He ordered, and then when she was gone he said, "Maybe it's too cold to ride in this weather."

She shook her head. "No, not too cold and not cold feet. There's some other reason, and I wish I could ask you what it is and why you came here. But you wouldn't tell me if I did. You're what John said: hardcase. But, Burt, I need a foreman. A foreman as hard as Buck Lake, and as mean. If I don't get one, I may go under."

"It's your battle, Nell," he said, and shrugged. "We all have to fight our own."

"So you're staying?"

"Indefinitely."

She mused over that one for a moment. "Indefinitely might be too long. This country won't be big enough for you and Buck now. Not after what happened today. You don't know Buck like I do. Did you ever see a man after his face had been stomped in with a boot heel? Eyebrows cut open, nose a bloody mass of torn flesh, teeth on the floor? I saw it once here a few months ago. I hope I don't have to see it again. And if Buck isn't enough, you've still got John to consider. He won't let you get away with killing that dog of his. So if you're going to stay, Burt, take that job with me."

"In other words," he said, "if I'm going to be killed for sticking around here I might as well help you before I do."

"You're hard," she answered from across the table. "You're as hard and ruthless as Buck and John. Maybe that's why I like you, because I'm a little hard myself, or so people

30

say. I was twenty years old when my father died and left me the Corley layout. A broken-down, booze-ridden old man left me a broken-down outfit and five broken-down hands to help run it. That was four years ago and the NC iron isn't that way now. It's a good outfit and I fought four years to make it so. Then a couple of years ago John came in and bought the Vinegarroon. He tried to buy me out but I wouldn't sell. So he began to play the devoted swain. He took me to dances. He even took me to church. He asked me for months to marry him, but Nellie wasn't buying any. I know John too well. He'd have combined the two spreads and pushed Mrs. Broadhurst into the kitchen with an apron on. Then he started putting on the pressure. Little things at first. Questioning the ownership of water-holes; forcing me to have my boundaries resurveyed. Things like that. And when my hands were in town, beating them up, forcing them to drift. There's a saying here in town that if you want to have your face changed, you need only go to work for Nell Corley. No, maybe you'd better not do it."

The waitress brought him a bowl of soup and he spread a napkin across his lap. Something about that appeared to amuse her, though she did not laugh. It was in her eyes.

He said, "Why don't you fight back at him the same way? Haven't you got lawyers and a sheriff here?"

She laughed at that one. "Tom Wade is an honest enough man and would be good for any county where there are no Broadhursts. Tom has one very bad fault: he hasn't got nerve. He's afraid of them. As for Caleb Sloane, he's the only lawyer in town, and he's Broadhurst's man. It was Cal who gave John the idea of homesteading four sections of my north range. Four touch punchers living in shacks a mile apart and working for John at the Vinegarroon; living on land I've always considered my range."

"No reason why you can't do the same thing," he reminded her.

"No reason at all," she answered softly, "except that

31

there's not a man in this country—with possibly one exception—with nerve enough to try it. He'd be shot at nights, burned out while he'was gone, and have his face stomped in Buck Lake. Last year a little ex-cowpuncher named Shorty Turner did that very thing, on his own. You should see what he looks like now since Buck got through with him. I witnessed it, and Buck got a ten-dollar fine for doing it. The shack is empty now. It will be for a long time to come."

She rose from the table and reached for her hat. "Well, I've got to go over and get a new dress fitted, now that Bedie has probably finished supper. If you stick around, drop by the NC sometime. It's six miles west of here, and I'm a good cook. So long, Burt . . . and be careful."

He told her so long and watched her slim, lithe figure go out through the arch and into the lobby. He finished his meal leisurely, paid the girl, and left. It was turning dark now and lights were on in a number of buildings along the cold street. The wind had died down but he knew that before morning it probably would be blowing a gale. There was a sign on the corner building that said *Prairie Saloon*, and he crossed the intersection, now deserted, and pushed through the swinging doors.

Chapter 5

THE BAR RANGED along the north wall and there were a number of tables for cards and dominoes and checkers. Two big stoves kept the place warm. He saw Broadhurst's big figure over at the opposite end of the bar, talking with another man, and stopped part way down. A few men were playing desultorily at the tables. They studiously continued as Howard waited for the bartender. He came over.

"Cigar," Burt said.

The man reached back of the bar and brought out two boxes. Burt selected a long panatella, bit off the end of it, and reached for a match. The bartender said significantly, "That'll be twenty-five cents, friend."

"I'm going to smoke part of it in here," Howard said. He lit it, puffed with a great show of satisfaction, and slid a quarter across the top.

The bartender dropped it into the till and Broadhurst came down and leaned an elbow on the bar, a small glass of rye in one fist.

"How was the room and supper?" he asked.

"No complaints," Burt answered.

"Drink?"

"Thanks. Not on top of supper."

"So you won't work for the Vinegarroon? Any special plans?"

Burt Howard looked at him. Three years now, come April. "Yes," he said, "I've got some very special plans."

The outer door banged and then the inner swinging doors

33

were pushed apart and a man came in. Howard instinctively turned his back away from the man, and he saw something he would never forget. The man stood five feet five, but except for his seedy clothes and run-down boots he didn't look much like a man. His right eyebrow had been torn down until it almost closed the eye. His nose was a flattened mass of cartilage and flesh. His mouth was twisted and some of his teeth gone. He looked around almost furtively, and then the bartender was down along the bar, moving fast and ominously.

"Get outa here, Shorty," he said harshly, pointing toward the door.

"I just come in to git warm, Joe," the other answered. "Kinda cold out."

"I said get the blazes out of here! I told you before not to come back in this place."

Burt Howard turned on the speaker. He eyed the bartender coldly. "It's a public place, isn't it?"

"Not for him, it ain't."

Broadhurst's amused voice broke in. "Better go a little easy, Joe. This is the hardcase who made things a little rough for Buck."

"I don't give a hoot who he is, John. It don't mean a thing in my life. He either gets out of here or I'll throw him through that door."

"You just go ahead and try it, mister," Burt Howard's voice softly. "Just make a move toward the end of that bar and I'll split your head open with the barrel of a six-shooter." And to Shorty: "Like a drink, mister?"

The smaller man came over, almost like a timid puppy. He looked at the scowling bartender and then up at Howard. "Sure would, mister."

"I'll have one with you," Burt answered. "I like one right after supper."

The drinks were brought and Burt poured for both of them. He put down the bottle and the little man lifted his

34

glass. "The name is Shorty Turner. Used to punch cows and homestead, but jobs are kind of tough to get these days. Maybe some day I can repay the favor. Here's health."

He drank, and Burt poured him another. Shorty Turner said, "Thanks. I'm sorta low on cash now, but I'll do the honors when I get back to work."

"I'm going to be around for a while," answered Howard. "Maybe I might help you find one. Meantime, here's ten dollars for expenses until you get going again. Pay me out of your first month's wages."

"I'll sure do it."

He took the money and scuttled out the door, because men were watching him and had seen a display of pity from this hardcase who had killed Broadhurst's bad dog, whipped Buck Lake, and backed down a tough bartender...all within a few hours after arriving in town.

John Broadhurst was looking at him, and there wasn't any amusement in the big man's eyes now. They were as brittle as cast-iron. He said, "You can't get away with it, Howard. You won't last in this town."

Howard sipped at the drink and took a drag on the panatella. "I'm not trying to get away with it. I just don't like being pushed around. I just don't like the idea of Lake giving me a face like Shorty Turner's."

"So Nell told you?"

Howard nodded. "She told me a lot of things."

"And offered you the job again?"

Burt Howard didn't answer. He was looking at the man, analyzing him, sizing him. up. It was the end of the trail for one of them and he knew it. He could kill Broadhurst now. Tell him who he was, about Delgadito, about the girl who had been on the stage that evening of the massacre at Henderson's ranch. He could lay open Broadhurst's scalp with a single blow of his gun barrel and then straddle him, slashing him across the eyebrows, bashing in his nose, and smashing his lips and teeth to a bloody, broken mass. Now

35

was the time to get the business over with and be on his way. But there was still the slightest possibility that it wasn't *the* John Broadhurst. And then there was the matter of Lake. They would say he had fled from Lake, the man who stomped in faces and who never forgot.

Burt Howard didn't answer the question. He finished off his drink.

"Didn't she?" insisted Broadhurst coldly.

"She did."

"And you're taking it?"

"Not unless I'm pushed into it," Howard said. "I don't like to be pushed around."

He turned on his heel and went out, into the cold of the deserted street, leaving the other man behind him, leaning against the bar. He went across to the hotel and up to his room and took writing paper and envelopes from one of the bags, and began writing a letter to old Al Tracy, over in Yuma.

> *Dear Al:*
> *Please take the letter I've enclosed and mail it in the post office. I've found my man. Say nothing to the Wells-Fargo people or anybody else. I'll handle it in my own way.*
>
> BURT

He addressed the envelope to Al Tracy, Yuma, Arizona, and then wrote another, sealed it, and addressed it, not neglecting to put on a stamp. He placed the second letter inside the one addressed to Al and then sealed the latter. He would mail it the following morning.

Meanwhile, after Howard had left, John Broadhurst remained leaning with an elbow on the bar. The bartender came over, corked the bottle, placed it on a shelf back of him, and picked up the two glasses.

"That boy," he said succinctly, "is tough, John. He's plenty tough."

36

"Maybe," the other said noncommittally.

The bartender dipped the two glasses in water, set them upside down on top of a wet rag, and then wiped at two wet spots on the bar.

"I don't know what he's got on his mind," he went on, still wiping, "but it's something. He don't look like no lawman, no Texas Ranger. He don't look like no saddle tramp. And any time you can take one of Buck's licks in the belly like he took and then bounce back like a rubber ball... well, you figure it out."

"I intend to, Joe," Broadhurst said, and put down his glass. "Be seeing you."

He went over to a chair and took a heavy coat from the back of it, slipping his heavy shoulders into the garment. He put on his cap and went out. He paused for a moment as though uncertain, looked at the lighted lobby of the hotel across the intersection of the two streets and down a way, and turned up the cross street.

He walked with the slow, thoughtful stride of a man who had something on his mind. It had been nearly three years now, come April, and so far there had been not the slightest sign of a repercussion. But the uneasiness, the fear of it, had been buried deep in his consciousness; a thing he had never been able to shake off completely. He walked along the boardwalk and then onto the hard dirt of the street, going back over events. He'd received advance notice from the Army on the day the rifles were to be shipped through, and by checking the manifests he had known that on the day they came through Hatrack the Old Woman Mine payroll was to be put aboard the stage in strongboxes. And it had been the rifles that had given him the idea of having the Apaches do the job. The reservation was close by Hatrack and the town was flooded with restless Indians almost every day. He had chosen Delgadito.

Naturally he had been sorry about Henderson and his wife and the kids. And he remembered the pretty girl he'd helped aboard the stage; the sole passenger. It had been too

37

bad about them all, for he had hoped that Delgadito and his men would perhaps kill only the guard and driver and herd the rest of them away until the ranch was burned. Too bad.

He remembered the investigation by Wells-Fargo men and the Pinkerton operatives, too. The report had been a clear case of Indian attack and massacre. But the uneasiness in his mind stemmed from the fact that such a report might have been a blind. They were clever, those men; they knew how to get at facts. Yet he had been careful to wait a few weeks before quitting his job. He had been careful to loaf around town for a few days before announcing that he was going *North*. He had been clever enough to buy his saddle horse and pack mounts from an out-of-the-way ranch before returning to the burned out ruins to pick up his spoils.

And now, after nearly three years, this hardcase had dropped into town. He didn't look like a lawman, a Texas Ranger. He had said, "I've got some very special plans," and a Wells-Fargo man or a Pinkerton operative wouldn't have said anything like that. They were quiet, unobtrusive.

And yet the uneasiness was there. The man didn't want a job. What *did* he want?

Chapter 6

HE CAME to a white picket fence and opened the gate, closing it behind him and moving up the walk to the low porch. The wind had died down now; only the cold bit at him. The stars were out, crystal clear in the winter sky. Maybe they wouldn't have that norther after all. Maybe it had blown itself out. Maybe... "Oh, heck!" Broadhurst muttered. "I'm thinking like an old woman," and knocked on the front door.

A voice called to come in and he twisted the knob and pushed. Just a girl he'd helped on the stage that day nearly three years ago, and now, for some strange reason, he couldn't get her out of his mind.

Two men were in the front room, seated in comfortable chairs before a glowing fire in the fireplace. Beside it, along the wall, was piled more of the dried mesquite wood, cut from the big pile out back of the house.

"Hello, John," Tom Wade greeted him, and rose from his chair, pushing back from the table which stood between himself and Caleb Sloane, the lawyer. "Come in and have a chair. Cold tonight, eh? Maybe our norther blew by."

"I hope so," Broadhurst answered, and removed his cap, then peeled out of the heavy coat. He went over to warm his hands at the fire as the sheriff drew up another chair.

Wade was possibly fifty, still blond and young-looking; a well built man of medium height not yet gone to seed. He slid the chair around near his own.

"Didn't know you had business, Tom," Broadhurst said, and sat down.

"No bother. Cal and me were just going over some papers. About through now. I've got a cold ride tomorrow to foreclose on Hinkley unless he raises some more money. Got to appear in court while Summers tries them two Mexicans for stealing chickens."

"Don't mind me," Caleb Sloane said. "I'll be leaving in just a moment."

He was possibly fifty-five, thin and stooped, with an oversized Adam's apple below a bony chin. He looked as though he hadn't had a square meal in months, though his appearance was very deceptive. Sloane was the type who couldn't have put on another pound of weight had he been a hotel chef.

"Not at all, not at all," Broadhurst murmured. "Matter of fact, I'm glad you're here, Cal. Where's Bedie?" he asked the sheriff.

"She went back downtown to the shop after supper to fit a new dress for Nell Corley. Don't tell me you came down to see *her?*"

"No," the other said, and took a cigar from the left breast pocket of his shirt. "Go ahead with your business, boys. I've plenty of time."

"No hurry," the lawyer said. "What's on your mind, John?"

"A little ruckus some stranger named Burt Howard caused when he hit town on the stage this afternoon."

Wade shifted in his chair and looked interested. "So I heard. Intended to go downtown after me and Cal finished and have a talk with him. So you lost Rex and Buck didn't make out so good? Howard, eh? Never heard of him."

"Neither did I. That's what I want you to find out. Where'd he come from? What's he doing here? How come he killed my dog, made a fool of Buck, and then backed down Joe the bartender at the Prairie Saloon on account of Shorty Turner? He's looking for trouble, Tom.'

"Tough, eh?"

"Hardcase clean through. Men like Joe don't back down, and he had a gun under the bar. But he didn't use it. He knew better. He backed down and served the drinks."

He went on to tell them in detail what had happened in the Prairie. Wade looked thoughtful.

He said, "We can't have that kind of thing going on in town. I'll haul him up in front of Summers in the morning for disturbing the peace by fighting in a public place."

"Whatever you say. Maybe Summers could find out a few things about him while trying him. Or ten days in jail while you backtrack on him."

Sloane cleared his throat, the prominent Adam's apple bobbing up and then down again.

"It's in your hands, of course, John. But as your lawyer I wouldn't advise it. We must bear in mind that you are not too—shall we say, well liked in this town by certain of the people, for various reasons. Nell Corley is a woman—a young and pretty woman—and public sympathy has naturally gravitated to her in this alleged fight you're having with her. That's always the case where a pretty woman is involved. Meantime, Shorty Turner is living here in town, on the streets every day, a constant reminder to these people of Buck's rather ruthless methods of handling the men who get in his way. If Summers fined Buck only ten dollars because of what happened to Shorty, it might not look so good if this stranger went to jail for his run-in with Buck in the hotel. We must think of these things."

Broadhurst ignored that one and looked at the sheriff. "Could you find out anything about him in ten days? Who is is? Where he came from? Why he's here? Strangers don't come in and make trouble like he did. I want to know things, Tom."

"You always have."

"Forget that. Can you do it?"

"I could try."

"Then arrest him," snapped back Broadhurst. "I don't

41

care what these people think. He shot my dog and I don't like it. He made a fool of Buck and of me too, and I don't like that either. Cal, you get a warrant for his arrest fixed up and I'll sign it. You serve it in the morning, Tom. No reason for you to kick. The county pays you to feed prisoners and you make a profit off them."

"I'm not kicking," the sheriff said noncommittally. "I'm just a county sheriff."

He got up and went to a glassed-in wall cabinet, the shelves loaded with ornamental dishes set on edge. He pulled open a lower door and brought out a bottle and glasses and soda. He came back and poured drinks for the three of them. The fire caved in suddenly and live coals rolled down on the hearth. Wade reshaped them with a poker, threw on two more sticks of mesquite wood, and sat down.

He picked up his glass. "Maybe he's on the dodge," he suggested.

"So much the better. That *is* an idea. He comes in and makes trouble five minutes after he hits town. So you go over and pick him up and jail him on suspicion. Come to think of it," he said, putting down his glass and leaning forward, "you do it tonight, Tom. No reason why the man who shot my dog and made this trouble should sleep in a warm bed at the hotel when he can share a cell with those two Mexican chicken thieves. Arrest him on suspicion—"

Footsteps sounded on the front porch and the door opened. Bedie Wade and Nell Corley came in. Nell carried a package under one arm.

"Hello, Pop," Bedie said, and went over and kissed him.

She put the package on the table, a slender girl just past twenty with blonde hair and hazel eyes. She began taking off her wraps, and Tom Wade's eyes followed her. She had been keeping house for him for five years now, since Mrs. Wade had died.

"You're back from the shop kinda early, ain't you?" he asked.

42

Nell laughed. "It was too cold down there to change for a fitting, Tom. So Bedie invited me up to stay all night and make the fitting here. Too cold to ride out to the ranch anyhow."

"All right," sighed the sheriff. "I guess that means we menfolk will have to skedaddle. I've got to go downtown anyhow."

Two pairs of feminine eyes swung to his face. Wade set down his glass, and a restraint in his manner told of a sudden uncomfortableness.

"How come, Pop?" Bedie asked. "Anything special? Mr. Broadhurst's visit up here wouldn't have anything to do with you going downtown in the cold to see a certain man named Burt Howard, would it?"

"Never mind, never mind. You take care of the house and your dress shop and I'll run the sheriff's office."

Nell Corley looked at Broadhurst, a smile that was sheer contempt on her pretty lips. "So you couldn't take it, could you? The great John Broadhurst couldn't stand to be humiliated in public and is sicking the law on a man who defended himself."

"Pop, you're not letting Mr. Broadhurst push you into something not on the level, are you?"

"No," grunted the sheriff doggedly. "I intended to have a talk with that fellow about what happened, anyhow. He can't come in here and disrupt the peace and expect to get away with it. For all we know he might be on the dodge, so I'm holding him until I find out. That's all."

"You're arresting him tonight?" demanded Bedie. "But according to what Nell told me he was only defending himself. If you're going to arrest somebody, who don't you arrest Buck for starting it?"

"I'm going to," Wade answered. "Just as soon as he shows up in town again."

"And old man Summers will fine him ten dollars which Mr. Broadhurst will pay."

43

Wade turned a stern eye on her. "Bedie," he said quietly, "you forget that Mr. Broadhurst is a visitor in this home and there's such a thing as manners. I'll hear no more of the matter."

It was a signal for them to go. They finished their drinks and put on their coats and the three of them went out into the night again, leaving the two women.

They walked down the hard-packed street in silence and came to the corner and stopped by the front door of the Prairie Saloon. Caleb Sloane said good night and made his way up the street. Broadhurst went inside the saloon. Tom Wade crossed the intersection cat-a-corner and went down to the big hotel. He entered the warm interior, and somehow he was glad that the place was deserted. He again felt that vague sense of uneasiness, he didn't know why. He wanted to say that it wasn't right; his inherent sense of honesty told him that it was very wrong. And he didn't know yet just why he was doing John Broadhurst's bidding. He owed the man nothing. He had won his three elections fairly and squarely. But this wasn't the first time the man had put on the pressure; and then, he told himself, he couldn't make an enemy of a man who was daily becoming more powerful. There was a house not paid for yet, and there was Bedie to think of.

Wade went over to the counter.

"Hello, Tom," the clerk greeted him. "We're all filled up. You'll have to go to another hotel. Anyhow, we do a strict cash business."

"Never mind. What room's this fellow Howard in?"

"That fellow who split Buck's feet apart until the bones cracked? He's up in eighteen. Going to arrest him?"

"Is he in?" Wade asked, ignoring the question.

"Yeah, come in a little while ago. From the Prairie. I hear he backed Joe down plenty when he wanted to throw Shorty Turner out in the street. I'll bet Joe don't think he's quite such a tough customer any more since—"

But Wade already was heading toward the carpeted stairs.

44

He went up, climbing easily, for he was still hard-muscled and strong. He turned past the banister and knocked on a door. Beneath it came a slit of yellow light.

"Come in," called a voice.

Wade opened and went in. The fire was burning in the stove and the room was warm. Burt lay on the bed, his boots off, a cigarette between his lips. He saw the badge adorning Wade's shirt front. One side of it had a nick in it. Tom Wade had been a deputy when an outlaw bullet, fired from ambush, had taken a nick from the badge and carried it into the former sheriff's heart.

Wade's eyes took in the man in his undershirt, propped up on a pillow at his ease; he observed the rather thin face, the long arms and powerful-looking hands. He was a good thirty pounds lighter than Buck Lake, the sheriff thought. He flicked a look at the gunbelt hanging on the head of the bedstead, at the bureau on top of which were writing materials, a pencil, a stamped and addressed letter, and a big, well padded leather money belt.

"Sit down," Burt invited.

Instead Wade crossed to the bureau and flicked open the belt. He saw gold notes, sheaves of them.

He closed the belt and turned. "All in hundreds?" he asked.

"Mostly. I've some smaller stuff mixed in."

"How much?"

"You'll be counting it anyhow."

Howard bent over enough to squash out the cigarette butt on the floor. Wade sat down straddle-legged across the chair, arms resting on the back.

"Howard, this afternoon you came in on the stage, and you wasn't in town two hours until you'd shot a dog, whipped a local man, and threatened a bartender with a gun. I think you'd better get up and put on your clothes."

"I see," Burt Howard murmured. "And you waited until sometime afterward before coming down, though word of it

45

was all over town within a few minutes. I just wonder if you've had any visitors tonight—somebody like John Broadhurst."

He got up to a sitting position, dropping his feet to the floor and reaching for a boot. Wade's face flushed.

"Never mind. Just get dressed and come along."

"How about bail?" Burt was grunting as he slid on the second boot and rose.

Wade shook his head.

"So Broadhurst wants me in the *carcel*, eh?" came the murmur.

"It's more than that, Howard. It might have been only disturbing the peace until I saw that money belt. Three weeks ago the stage was held up a hundred miles north of here and a shipment of money for the Carterville Bank stolen. Twenty-five thousand dollars, most of it in hundred-dollar denominations. Gold-backs. The job was done by a lone man who was masked. I'll have to hold you for investigation until I backtrack."

He wanted to ask the man about the fight, but there was something in this hardcase's manner that said it wouldn't do much good. Wade went over and picked up the gunbelt as Burt finished dressing and put on his heavy mackinaw and cap. He took the money, and Burt picked up the letter and shoved it in his pocket.

"I'd like to mail this on the way down," he said.

They went downstairs and down the street. It led past the frame post office, and Wade waited while his prisoner slid the envelope through a slot in the front door.

They went on toward the jail.

Chapter 7

THE JAIL was a low structure of red sandstone hauled from a distant mountain, as was the courthouse nearby. Both edifices sat back on the prairie about one hundred yards from the main street, as though Carterville's citizenry knew that some day the town would expand enough to cut a second street through in front of the county buildings. Howard and the sheriff walked over, cutting across a vacant lot between a store and saddle shop.

They came up in front of the iron door and Wade took a large key from his pocket and opened it. He opened a second, barred door with the same key, and nodded for Burt Howard to go in.

Most of the other county officers had their offices over in the courthouse close by, but from the desk and other things in a corner Howard knew that the sheriff did his business from here. A wall of bars ran across the room from floor to ceiling, with a door in the center. Back of the bars were three large cells, with ample space for a "bull pen." Wade saw two Mexicans lounging on benches by a stove in a corner of the bull pen. The interior was newly white-washed and didn't have the odor usually associated with jails; sheep dip in particular, for sanitation.

Wade sad, "Sit down over there," and locked the inner door. He came over carrying Burt Howard's gunbelt, which he hung on a peg in a corner. He took the money belt from a pocket of his heavy coat and laid it on the desk and sat down, reaching for pen and a booking form.

"Nothing personal in this, Howard," he said, and wrote down the name "Burt Howard." "Age?"

"Twenty-nine."

"Home?"

"Carterville, Texas."

The sheriff wrote it down and then rested his pen. "All right, Howard; if that's the way you want it, that's the way it'll be. I don't like to hold a man in jail when it can be avoided. Anything you'd like to tell me about yourself?"

"Nothing."

"Are you on the dodge?"

"You won't find my face on any reward posters."

"What about this money here, a lot for a man to be packing around?"

"What about it?" came back the brittle reply.

Wade sighed and reached for the belt. He opened it and took out the sheaves of gold notes and began to count. Howard smoked a cigarette and said nothing, lolling in the chair. The two Mexicans stood at the bars, eyes on the two men and the money. Wade finished counting. He put the money back into the belt, went to a safe and dialed. When the door had been slammed shut again he came back and sat down.

"Eighteen thousand, nine hundred and fifty-five dollars. That check with your figures?"

"Just about."

Wade scribbled on a clean sheet of paper, signed his name blotted the ink, and handed it over. "A receipt for the money. What became of the rest of the twenty-five thousand?"

"There was only twenty thousand, all told."

But the sheriff shook his head. "That won't get you anywhere, Howard. The bank and the Wells-Fargo people know how much was on that stage. But I want to be fair. Tomorrow morning I'm sending a deputy to the railhead to get in touch with the Wells-Fargo people by telegraph, and they'll have men down here in no time to check up on you.

48

They'll be here in not more than three days. Pinkerton men. I said I want to be fair. If you're not guilty, I could send another to the people you got that money from."

"There wasn't any telegraph station around where I got that money," Burt Howard said.

And that was true. The bank from which he'd drawn the money was not serviced by a railroad.

No, Burt Howard thought, this is my hand and I'll play it my own way. Let them think what they please. This is Broadhurst's work and I'll bide my time.

It was the hardcase in him, and the sheriff seemed to realize it too. He opened a drawer of his desk and put in the filled-out booking form. "Take all the stuff out of your pockets and put it on the desk. Keep your tobacco, papers, and matches."

Burt obeyed, and when the contents of his pockets were on the desk Wade saw that there was no money except a few silver coins.

"That all the other loose cash you've got? You're going up in front of Tobe Summers in the morning. He's JP here. Ten dollars fine for disturbing the peace, half of which Tobe gets, plus his fifty a month salary. Here, let me give you the money to pay it."

He reached for a hip pocket and Burt Howard's voice said dryly, "I'll probably be here ten days anyhow while you investigate me, perhaps the sentences can run concurrently. Thanks, but I never accept favors from strangers."

Wade grunted and rose to his feet, bending over the stuff Burt had laid out on top of the desk. He shoved across a pocket comb, then separated the three or four dollars in silver from the other stuff and shoved that across too.

"You'll need money for smoking tobacco and such," the sheriff grunted. "I'll bring what you want from the store ever noon when I come back from dinner. Okay, you can have that end cell."

He took a key ring and unlocked the door. Burt went in

and walked to the cell. The blankets were clean and fresh.

"Mucho dinero, señor,"—much money, mister—one of the Mexicans said. *"Usted habla Español?"*

It was their way of opening conversation.

"I speak it fairly well," Burt answered. "What are you in here for?"

The other shrugged. "We are two poor sheepherders wintering here from the cold and doing odd jobs to keep the stomach from becoming much hungry. But there is not much work and we are hungry ... and this man has many pullets—*pollos*—So what matter that he loan us a few? You understand, mister. What are you in for?"

"I am a bank robber," Burt said dryly, and went to the stove to warm himself.

"Oyez!" (Hear ye!) This man robs the bank and has much money and we rob only the chicken pens. When we get out we shall become bank robbers."

Wade was busy putting the rest of the contents of Burt's pockets into a small sack. He placed them in a drawer and came over to the cell.

"I'll be down in the morning about seven. We sweep out this place every morning and make up the bunks. Once a week we scrub this place from floor to ceiling. Bedie, my daughter, will bring over breakfast for these two hombres. I'll take you to the restaurant for your meals, unless I'm busy. See you in the morning."

He went out, locking the inner barred door and then the outer steel door behind him. He walked thoughtfully over toward the Prairie, a slight frown on his brow as though he were thinking heavily. Like John Broadhurst he was puzzled.

He pushed into the warmth of the Prairie's interior and ordered a cigar. Broadhurst got up from a checker game and came over. "Get him all right?" he asked.

Wade nodded glumly, biting at the cigar.

"What do you think?"

"Name, age, and address. The address is Carterville, Texas. I expect he's figuring on sticking around."

"So I see. And that's all?"

"He had twenty thousand, lacking a thousand or so, in gold notes on him."

Broadhurst's eyebrows went up. "Whew! That kind of dinero? No wonder he wasn't in any hurry to go to work."

"All in hundreds, except some smaller stuff. I'm sending Poke Stanton to the railhead early in the morning to wire Wells-Fargo to bring a man down to check the serial numbers on those bills. Buchannan, at the bank, doesn't have them."

Broadhurst's expression didn't change, but all of a sudden he was seeing that girl he'd lifted on the stage, pretty certain she was going to her death, and the old fear hit at him from within. Wells-Fargo had cleared the matter, but you could never tell about them and their Pinkerton men. Three years now, come April. And after that stage holdup of a few weeks back, he knew that somewhere in the country Pinkerton men were still on the trail. That was why some of his men always tried to be around the Wells-Fargo office when the stage arrived. It was one reason he had bought the best hotel in town: to keep a check on new arrivals. Of course, there was a lot of difference between a holdup in this section of the country three or four weeks back and a massacre of nearly three years ago hundreds of miles away. But his was the uneasiness of a man who had done wrong and that uneasiness was upon him now.

"Why all the bother, Tom?" he asked casually. "They can wire you the numbers and it will be an easy matter to check them."

"That's up to them," Wade replied, and changed the subject. "I want you to have Buck and Kansas and Luke in town by ten in the morning, and you don't have to ask why."

"I've already sent word out to the ranch. They'll be here. We've got to keep law and order."

The door opened and a man came in, staggering a little. He wore worn chaps and boots, gunbelt, and had a very ragged sweater stretched over the outside of at least three wool shirts. His battered Stetson covered a cloth that had been pulled down over his ears and tied under his bony chin. He hadn't shaved in a week.

He rocked up to the bar and gave the scowling Joe a silly grin. "I wanta double snort of one hundred proof. I been ridin' and I'm cold. Who wants to hire a real rip-snortin', rawhide cowpuncher? I can ride any horse that ever hit the ground on four feet an' lick any man that ever walked on two feet. That's me, Jeb Stuart, an' I ain't no kin to no generals."

Joe poured him a big slug into a water glass and said coldly, "That'll be thirty cents, mister."

The saddle tramp picked up the glass and downed its contents in a single gulp, then slapped the empty back on the bar. It fell over and rolled off the back edge and broke on the floor. The puncher wiped at his lips with a sleeve.

"Take it outa my first month's pay when I git a job," he said.

"I'll take it outa your hide," Joe snarled, and made for the end of the bar.

Wade said, "Hold it, Joe!" sharply.

He looked at the other, his eyes brittle. "Pay up, mister," he ordered.

"Ain't got it and won't have it till I git me a job. What's the matter with you fellers. Cain't you trust a man—"

Wade already had stepped close and slipped the other's gun from its worn sheath. He shoved him toward the door. "Get going," he ordered. "Over to the jail."

He got the reins of the broken-down cow pony and led it over, paying no attention to the voluble protests of his prisoner. The man was reeling a bit now from the final double slug, and once he stumbled and fell sprawling. Wade locked him in a cell to himself, saw the man tumble on top of the bunk, still in boots and chaps, and begin to snore. The sheriff went outside. He mounted the pony, rode it to the livery to be put up for the night and fed, and returned home.

He opened the back door and went in, and as he started through the kitchen to the front room he heard a squeal and caught a glimpse of Nell Corley in petticoat and stockinged feet making a dash for the bedroom. Bedie's laughter rolled out and rose higher at the look on her father's face.

"Maybe I better come back later," Wade suggested, red-faced.

"It's all right, Pop. We'd just finished the fitting and she was getting ready to dress. You can stay."

Nell came out wearing one of Bedie's long robes and sat down at the fire. She said, laughing, "I'm a very modest young woman, Tom, even if some people in this town don't think so."

"Don't mind me," he said wearily. "I'm just a broken-down old codger, not much good even for sheriffing any more, looks like."

"What about Burt?" Nell asked, and their quick glances at her use of his first name didn't escape her.

Wade told them what had happened, of the money, of his offer to pay the fine.

"Of course he wouldn't take it," Nell said. "I told you he's hardcase. I know that Buck thinks he's a pretty bad boy around town, but I've got a very strong hunch that if Buck has any sense he'll let Burt alone. That man will kill and kill quick, if he's pushed too far. And he warned Broadhurst that he didn't like to be pushed.

"And," she added thoughtfully, after a pause, "that gives me an idea."

Chapter 8

HOWARD WOKE up early the following morning to the sound of loud groans coming from the center cell. It was cold in the jail and he stretched an arm from beneath the covers to look at his watch. Six-fifteen. He looked over at the new arrival, who sat on the edge of his bunk, hands to his face, letting out more groans.

"Tough night, eh?" he asked.

The other staggered to his feet and turned, grabbing at a bar to steady himself. "Oh, Lordy!" he groaned, and staggered to the water pail.

He didn't quite make it. There was a latrine in the cell, its sewer pipes leading to a cement-covered deep well that had been dug out back. The puncher leaned over it and began to retch. When he turned his face was pale.

"I oughta kill that Mexican sheepherder, no matter what his good intentions," he mumbled. "Stopped off yesterday late to have supper with that herder at his wagon. He offered to let me stay all night, but I wanted to come on into town, so the son of a gun gimme a pint of raw mezcal to keep me warm on the ride in. I drunk it all and—"

He went for the latrine again. Then he straightened and dipped a big tin cup of icy water, gulping it and then another. Then he went down in a heap and the back of his head struck the concrete floor. The shock of the cold water in his tortured vitals had knocked him cold.

Burt got up and dressed. There was nothing he could do for the unfortunate saddle tramp, since the man's cell door

54

was locked. The fire was banked and Burt Howard shoveled out all the ashes into a bucket, put in fresh wood, and began to make up his bunk. By the time he and the Mexicans had the place swept out and clean, the other prisoner had come to and was sitting on his bunk, moodily smoking a cigarette.

"The sheriff will be over in a few minutes to take us to breakfast," Howard said. "You get a few cups of black coffee down you and you'll feel better. My name is Burt Howard."

"Mine's Jeb Stuart," the other said, shaking hands through the bars. "As of now I'm plumb swearing off liquor . . . but I'd give my saddle for a good snort right now."

Presently the front door rattled and opened and Wade opened the second, inner door with the bars. He came in and nodded a good morning, and looked at the picture of misery sitting on the bunk.

"I won't ask how you feel," he said. "I know."

"I don't need to tell you either, Sheriff. I know it too. Guess I musta made pretty much of a fool of myself last night, though things are kinda hazy. Where'd you pick me up?"

Wade told him, unlocking the door and then coming in to open the cell. He went to a cabinet and brought out clean towels and soap and gave them to the four men. Presently there was a tap on the front door and Wade opened it to let in Bedie, carrying two miner-type lunch pails and a brown jug of steaming coffee. Burt Howard instinctively rose to his feet as she gave the food to her father. He carried it in to the two Mexicans and then nodded at Howard and Stuart.

"You boys come along and we'll go over to the hotel for breakfast. Or there's a quieter place down the street a ways, if you don't want to be stared at. But the ham and eggs are better at the Broadhurst."

"Then lead me to 'em, Sheriff," Stuart said. "I've had four meals in three days."

Wade said, "Bedie, this is Burt Howard and Jeb Stuart. Men, my daughter, Bedie Wade."

55

Burt saw the clear hazel eyes and knew that they were probing him though not appearing to do so, and he somehow knew in that moment that she was aware of her father's inherent fear of Broadhurst and his men; that it was a wound deep within her, a secret she shared only with herself.

They went outside into the biting cold of the early morning, the three men walking downtown. Wade might not have had as much nerve as he should have had, but when they passed the Prairie he showed himself to be a man of understanding. "In that door," he said. "The county will pay for the drink, Stuart. And I'll pay for the one you didn't pay for last night."

"Now I remember," Stuart chuckled. "It's all coming back. I cert'nly must made a prize mule outa myself last night. Whoosh!"

"You didn't do so badly," the sheriff answered cryptically as they pushed inside.

There was a day bartender on duty, and after Stuart had had his shot of "hair of the dog that bit me" the three of them went over into the hotel dining room and took the same table in a corner where Howard had eaten the night before.

"Where'd you come from, Stuart?" Tom Wade asked as they waited.

"Little of everywhere. I worked up in Wyoming Territory this summer for a horse outfit, but I don't like snow, so I drifted south for the winter. If I'da knowed it was this cold down here and jobs so scarce, I'da shore gone some other direction. Any chance of a job around here—after I serve out my jail sentence?"

"Possibly. We'll have a spring roundup coming on. John Broadhurst has a pretty big iron and might use some men. He offered Howard here a job last night. Don't know about Nell Corley. She tried to hire him too. I'll look around and see what I can do."

"I'd be much obliged. I'm tired of riding the grub line."

Burt Howard liked the man. Stuart was a different man

this morning, despite his ragged, unshaved appearance. His face was long and bony and his teeth protruded enough in front to give his mouth a somewhat humorous expression, indicating a nature that didn't take too heavily the vicissitudes of life.

A waitress came up with three glasses of water and Burt heard a woman's voice say, "Good morning, Mr. Howard. How are you?"

He looked up into the pretty face of Mrs. Clay.

"You didn't lose much time," he smiled. "You found your folks all right?"

"The driver of the rig knew where they live. No, I didn't lose much time. My dad told me about a job here and I came right down last evening to get it. You see, I have a daughter to support and he doesn't make much working at the livery. I'd like to thank you again for saving Margaret from that dog yesterday. I'll never be able to repay you. If there's anything I can ever do for you, Mr. Howard, just ask me."

"There's a dog-goned pretty woman," Stuart remarked, watching as she headed for the kitchen to give their orders to the cook. "Who is she?"

Burt told him. Wade hadn't said anything. He sat smoking a cigarette. Presently she came back with two platters of ham and eggs and fried potatoes, and carrying in her other hand a pitcher of hot coffee. Nell Corley had come through the archway from the lobby and was threading her way among the tables. She sat down and said to Wade, "Bedie makes the best coffee in the world, Tom, next to mine, but I wanted another cup while I looked over the criminal. Good morning, jail bird."

Howard told her good morning and Wade sat looking at Mrs. Clay when she placed the orders on the table.

He said, "So you're the woman whose baby was attacked by Broadhurst's dog?"

"Yes, I am, Sheriff. And if it hadn't been for Mr. Howard here, we'd be burying my baby this afternoon. I owe a debt

57

that I can never repay, and if there's anything I can ever do for him, all he has to do is just ask."

Burt Howard felt Nell Corley's eyes upon him and he felt uncomfortable. Those eyes were too frank and appraising... and slightly amused. When Mrs. Clay was gone Nell looked at him more closely.

"That's a pretty generous offer from a lovely young widow, Burt. And I've also heard they make the best wives. I'd look into it, if I were you... after you get out of jail."

She laughed at his tightened lips and silence as he bent over his plate, and then she looked at Jeb Stuart. "Who're you?" she asked.

"Me? I'm just a pore, lonesome, busted-down cowhand what got hisself all tangled up with the law, ma'am. I got a hangover, too. Now if you'll excuse me I'm a-goin' to dive into these ham an' eggs. I ain't et much lately."

She said no more, drinking her coffee while the conversation drifted to the weather, the coming spring roundup, and other local topics. Wade sat smoking, silently thoughtful.

At ten o'clock that morning the front doors of the jail rattled again and Tom Wade came in, followed by a deputy, a shortwinded, fat man of perhaps sixty whose name was Bill Stovers. The four men—Howard, Jeb Stuart, and the two Mexican sheepherders—went out, followed by the two lawmen. They crossed the short distance to the front door of the low building of red sandstone and stepped onto the concrete porch. Around the front door lounged a few men, smoking and waiting. Burt saw Buck Lake, Kansas, and the man Luke, talking with Broadhurst.

Lake's eyes, meeting his own briefly, were hard and penetrating, but no greetings passed between them.

Wade said, "All right, boys. Put out your cigarettes and let's go inside. Tobe'll be along any minute now."

They passed into a hallway on either side of which were the various offices of county officials. At the rear end of the hallway, through double doors, was the courtroom. A gray-haired man with a dewlap under his freshly shaven chin came out of an office with the letters *County Judge* painted on the door, and Wade introduced him as Judge Burns.

"He tries some of the cases here," Wade explained to Burt, "and there's really no need for a JP. But Tobe has to make a living somehow, and he can relieve the judge of a lot of petty stuff."

Well, Burt Howard thought, as they entered the courtroom, that's some consolation. I'm glad my case is petty.

There was grim irony in the thought.

About thirty or forty people already were in the room, most of them standing close to a big stove in a corner not far from the judge's bench. Wade nodded toward a bench and the two Mexicans filed in and sat down, followed by Stuart and Howard, Lake and his companions pushed in and sat down.

"Git the hangman's rope," Stuart said humorously. "It won't be long now till the jury brings in a verdict."

Tobe Summers came in through a door back of the judge's bench, from a room that was supposed to be the judge's "chamber." There had been a window back of the bench, too, when the courthourse originally was built. This had been hurriedly removed and filled in with stone at the orders of the district judge, who wanted solid stone at his back while trying murder cases. The judge, it appeared, was a cautious man.

Summers was in his late sixties, a bony, toothless man who drank his whiskey straight and boasted about his aristocratic Southern ancestry. He wore a slouch hat, sweater, wool pants, and a pair of worn brogans. His gray mustache was the "splay puss" type, and he hadn't shaved in three days. His bloodshot eyes gave some indication why.

His Honor had been on another bender.

"He said, "Mornin', fellers, this courtisnowinsession,"

59

and sat down, dropping the hat on the floor beside his chair. "Hurry up and get settled. What's the first case?"

The first case, after the spectators had seated themselves, involved the two Mexicans accused of stealing chickens. Wade beckoned to the two men and the Mexicans, now a little nervous, rose and stood before the bar of Carterville's justice of the peace.

Wade rose and stood beside them. "Judge Summers, night before last Lem Potter heard his chickens making quite a racket and went out with his shotgun, thinking it was a polecat in the coop. He found these two men and held them at gun point and then herded them over to my house. I locked them up. Lem's already told you the circumstances; he couldn't appear today because he's out working in six heifers he just bought, bringing them from the Wagon Wheel to his section out of town.

Summers looked at the two culprits.

"What's your names?"

A shrug of two pairs of shoulders. *"No entiendo, Señor Jefe."*

"Talk English!"

More shrugs.

"Do you plead guilty or not guilty?"

Two more shrugs. A ripple of laughter went through the courtroom and Tobe Summers glared.

"Does anybody here in this court speak Spanish?" Tobe said angrily.

Burt Howard let a faint grin come over his face and nudged Stuart as he started to rise. Jeb relaxed and nobody answered. There was just that increasing ripple of laughter going through the courtroom. Burt heard a lusty laugh and saw Nell Corley, sitting with Bedie Wade. Nell had her handkerchief to her mouth, stifling laughter that bubbled up.

"Now looka here," the judge said sharply, shooting a glance nothing short of baleful around the room. "I'll have no funnin' here in this court." And to the Mexicans: "I find you two guilty as charged and sentence you to thirty days in the county jail."

He held up his outspread hands to indicate ten, then held them up twice more and pointed in the direction of the nearby jail.

One of the Mexicans broke into fluid Spanish, addressing Tobe and speaking volubly, the words pouring from his tongue. He gesticulated, postulated, he ended in a bow before Tobe, who had understood not a word.

Jeb Stuart shot a sidewise grin at Howard, nudged him with an elbow, and rose.

"Your Honor," he said in a lazy drawl, while Howard fought down laughter, "he says that he took it for granted that you would find them guilty and he wants to thank you for the verdict. He says as how it's cold, they have no money and no jobs, and now you, outa the kindness of your heart, have made it possible for them to have a nice warm place to stay where they can have plenty of good grub, sleep all they want to, and play cards. He says as how he thanks you from the bottom of his heart. He was afraid you'd turn 'em loose."

Jeb sat down again, and even Tom Wade's face relaxed into a smile as more laughter arose from the spectators. The Mexicans returned to their seats and Wade called Buck Lake's name. Summers said, "Kansas, you and Luke might as well come on up too. You're charged with fighting in a public place and disturbing the peace. How do you plead: guilty or not guilty?"

"Make it easy on yourself," Lake grunted contemptuously.

"I could make it hard on you," Tobe Summers snapped back. "For two cents I'd sentence you to thirty days in the county jail just to show you that you cain't bluff everybody in this town. But because you got yourself licked good and proper by that stranger, I'll make it ten dollars apiece. Pay up. Ten dollars or ten days."

61

Lake took a crisp bill from his pocket and tossed it to the judge. Kansas and Luke followed suit. They started to turn away, to leave the court, but Summers' voice stopped them.

"Just a minute, Buck, you and the other two," the JP said softly. "You came into this court packin' guns when you knowed very well I don't allow it. That'll be five dollars apiece more for contempt of court."

They paid off, sullenly this time, and in the face of more laughter. Tobe pocketed the money with obvious satisfaction and called, "Next case, Jeb Stuart."

Stuart got up and ambled over in front of His Honor. "Guilty," he drawled.

"Guilty of what?" snorted Tobe. "I ain't ast you yet, have I?"

"Well, you're a-goin' to, so I just thought I'd save you the time. Drunk and disturbing the peace."

"Got ten dollars?"

"Nope," Stuart replied cheerfully.

"Then—"

"Just a minute, Tobe, I have," called a voice.

All eyes in the court turned as Nell Corley got up and came over. She looked at Stuart, sizing him up. "You looking for a job?" she asked.

"Yessum, I reckon I could use one."

"You're hired. How much, Tobe?" She was opening her purse.

"Now just a minute, Nell," Tobe Summers put in. "Who's runnin' this court, you or me?"

"I could do a better job of it," she said. "But I'm a ranch woman. You go ahead and run it. Here," handing him a gold eagle.

"All right. Seein' as how it's you, I'll dismiss the case. Case dismissed. And, young feller, from now on when you go into a bar be dog-goned sure you can pay for the drinks you order. Next time I see you up in front of me it won't be no ten dollars. It'll be ten days. Next case."

Burt rose leisurely. He was pretty certain what was coming. He could see it in her eyes, in the way she waited. He could let her pay his fine and go to work for her, after turning down the offer of a job the night before. But she was overlooking the fact that Wade was holding him as a suspected road agent. Tobe Summers peered down from the bench.

"So you're this Burt Howard, heh?"

"I'm Burt Howard."

The whole proceedings bored him. It was all tinny, cheap tinsel; a bright, small-town glitter he wanted to have over and done with, so he could get at the job he'd spent three years and come hundreds of miles to do. He wasn't worried about the money. The Pinkerton men working for Wells-Fargo could establish very quickly the fact that he hadn't held up the stage and taken the money. A few days in jail, while Tom Wade waited for the Pinkerton men to arrive, meant nothing. His one fear was that they might discover something about Broadhurst that would deprive him, Burt Howard, of the opportunity of squeezing the life blood out of Broadhurst, turning him into a shaking hulk of fear.

"Get on with the case," he told Tobe Summers impatiently and in a toneless voice. "I shot that bad dog of Broadhurst's. I had a little ruckus with this fellow they call Buck Lake, which didn't amount to much. I'm guilty and I haven't got the money to pay my fine."

Two voices spoke up in unison. They said, "I have."

Burt turned to see Broadhurst and Nell Corley eyeing each other. "Well, now," Tobe Summers said sarcastically, "this is most interestin'. I knowed the ranches around here was short of hands, but I didn't think it was so bad that owners had to start bidding against each other for jailed men."

The Corley woman ignored that one. She looked at Burt. "That offer of a job is still open. Foreman. I understand, Burt, that you're a suspected road agent. I don't believe that either. I'll pay your fine and go any bail you need if you'll go to work for me."

"Howard looks like a good man, Tobe," Broadhurst said heavily. "I'll be needing good men for the spring roundup. Of course, if he's guilty of being the road agent who held up the stage, that's different. But I'll take the gamble. If he'll go to work for me at the ranch I'll top Nell's offer and pay him better wages."

Tobe scratched his whiskery chin and looked down at Burt. "Which one you aimin' to go to work for?" he asked.

"I didn't say I wanted to work for either."

"Particular, eh?"

"Very particular."

"Where'd you come from?"

"Bronson, on the stage."

"Live there?"

"I live in Carterville."

"Hm. Tell you what I'm a-goin' to do: You shot that dog and saved a baby's life, the way I hear it. It was Buck and Kansas and Luke who picked that ruckus with you. I never liked Joe anyhow and I wish you'da bent a gun barrel over his ornery skull. I'll dismiss the charges against you if you'll go to work for Nell. She's short of good men."

"I don't like being pushed around."

"So I heard. Did you hold up that stage three weeks ago?"

"No. The money came from the sale of my ranch over in Arizona. I got it from a bank in a town called Hatrack."

So it was out. Broadhurst would know, or suspect, that no mere coincidence had brought him here to Carterville. That was the way Burt wanted it. He wanted to plant uneasiness and fear in the big man's mind. And that was the way it was going to be. Burt Howard didn't look at Broadhurst; he could imagine what was going on in the mind of the other, and the thought was a tonic.

He added, "The Wells-Fargo people have the serial

numbers of the money taken in the stage holdup. It will be an easy matter to check. I'll stay in jail until the sheriff can satisfy himself."

Tobe rubbed his chin again. "What're you doin' here in Carterville?"

"That's my own business."

"Hmmm. Reckon it is at that. Case dismissed. Tom, you can take over the prisoners."

He got up, and that meant that court was adjourned. Howard walked over to the stove to warm his hands, ignoring Nell and Broadhurst and the others. Shorty Turner limped up and stuck out his hands. His smashed and battered face was all smiles, the smiles of a gargoyle, for Shorty's face was a horrible-looking sight. And the man who had done it stood within a few feet of them.

"Glad he let you go," the little puncher said. "I'm yer friend."

"Thanks, Shorty. I might need one. Stick around a few minutes."

He went over to Nell Corley, nodding to Bedie. Broadhurst said, "So you're sticking around for a while, eh?"

"I am."

"So you're from Arizona? This place called Hatrack?"

Howard looked at him, at the impassive face, the strength and indomitable will back of it, and wondered what John Broadhurst was thinking. The two had never met before the coming of Burt Howard to Carterville, for his ranch had lain far to the south of Hatrack and he'd seldom gone there. He had done no business with the bank there until the sale of his ranch and subsequent deposit of the proceeds. This was some time after Broadhurst had quit his job and left to pick up the money taken in the massacre.

No, he thought, he doesn't know me or the name, but he's uneasy.

"Hatrack," Howard said casually. "I bought a ranch

65

there, ran it for a few months, and sold out. Ever been there?"

Broadhurst shook his head. "Just curiosity. I've heard a lot about that Arizona country."

"It's heat, dust, desert, and Apaches. They're getting pretty well whipped out now, except for an occasional raid."

"I've heard the climate is a lot healthier over there, Howard. Much more than here." Broadhurst said it casually, though there could be no mistaking his meaning.

Howard's eyes froze. He said, "That's the third time I've been pushed, mister."

He turned to Nell Corley. "Is that job still open?"

"You're hired."

"Foreman? Run the place my way and hire and fire who I wish?"

"That's a foreman's job."

"Shorty, come over here. You're working for the NC now. You and Jeb get a rig from the livery. Pick up my saddle bag and war bag at the Wells-Fargo office, and get my stuff from the hotel room and take it out to the ranch. I'll be out as soon as I get clear of the sheriff."

He went over to the two Mexicans, who were being herded back toward the jail by a deputy, and joined them. The courtroom emptied and Tom Wade found himself alone with Broadhurst.

"You've made an enemy and a downright bad one, John," the sheriff said uneasily.

"I was afraid he'd take the hint and leave," Broadhurst said. "I want him to stick around for a while. I want to find out a few things."

"I don't want any trouble," Wade said quickly, and his reply showed the uneasiness and fear he felt.

"You just run the sheriff's office, Tom. I'll take care of my own affairs."

He went out into the cold sunlight and nodded to Kansas. He spoke in a low voice.

"Kansas, you go back to the ranch and take a good horse and a pack mount. You know where Dave Bell is holed up. Tell that horse thief gun fighter to look me up at the ranch. Bring him in at night and keep him holed up in the ranch house out of sight of the other men."

Chapter 9

LATE THE FOLLOWING afternoon the front doors of the jail clanged, and Howard, busy drawing two cards to three kings, didn't look up. Wade had come to take him to supper. He drew the two cards, masked his disappointment, and put out four matches into the pile in the middle of the cell bunk.

"Burt, we'll know in a minute," Wade's voice called. "I got a telegram here that the stage driver brought in from the railhead. Wells-Fargo said there was no reason to send down a man until I checked the serial numbers on that money taken from the holdup with what you've got."

"All right," Howard said, and laid down his hand.

He grinned and picked up the pile of matches, listening to the stream of disgusted Spanish, and nodding. The *Americano* had won again. He shuffled the deck, and presently the door leading through to the sheriff's office opened and Wade came in.

"You can pick up your things, Burt," Wade said. "You told the truth, all right. There's your money and gunbelt and the rest of the stuff on the desk. Count the money and give me back my receipt."

Howard counted it, passed over the receipt, and unloosened his belt, lifting his shirt tail. He buckled on the belt and rearranged his clothes into place.

"That's a lot of money to be packing around," the sheriff observed. "It might tempt people. We've got a good bank here."

"I'll be my own banker," Burt Howard said, and slung his gunbelt into place beneath the coat.

They went out into the late evening air, which was still wintry and still bitingly cold, and down to the main street, neither not saying much. Bedie Wade came along the boardwalk, a sack of groceries in her arms.

"Pop, I'm late tonight, but I'll hurry home and fix the Mexicans' supper. I'll just have to warm up the stew and fix coffee. How are you Burt?"

"He's free," the sheriff said. "It was somebody else held up the stage. How about coming along home for supper with us, Burt?"

He saw the sincerity in the man's face, the welcome in Bedie's eyes, and he thought that she must get pretty lonesome keeping house for her father and working in her small shop.

He said, "Thanks, but I'd better get a rig and go out to the ranch tonight. You'll have to tell me how to get there."

Wade told him and, later, Burt Howard drove west from town, following a well-worn road that dipped in and out with the undulating swell of the prairies. He crossed a creek, its bed now dry gravel and sand, three miles from town and just as dusk began to come down, trotting and walking the team by turns. He pushed them through a forest of mesquites and into a gully, pulled up the cut bank on the opposite side and went on. After a time lights showed like pin points, far in the distance.

He noted the lay of the land, the cowman in him watching for a cow and calf here and there, bedded down against the cold, dark blots in the darkness. Spring roundup wasn't too many weeks off, and he'd have his work cut out for him.

Presently the dark outlines of the buildings loomed up and he pulled up close by a corral. He got down stiffly, beating his gloved hands against his sides to increase circulation. A door opened, throwing a square of yellow light onto the earth, and a man's voice called, "Who is it?"

"Burt Howard, Shorty. Give me a hand with the team."

Shorty came hurrying out, putting on a heavy coat, and went to work on the traces. "Got out all right, huh?" the broken little puncher asked.

"All clear. Where do we put them? You can take them back to the livery in the morning."

Afterward they went together to the bunkhouse, a frame building of two stories that once had been a residence. They crossed the porch and entered the living room. Burt saw four other men besides Jeb lounging around a stove. From the kitchen came the rattle of dishes. Howard let the gaze of the curious four play over him, then went into the kitchen. The cook, a cigarette dangling from his lips, was drying dishes. He was a blond, angular youngish man of twenty-three or so.

"Got anything left over from supper?" Howard asked.

The cook grunted sourly. "I reckon. Looks like you coulda got here—"

"Fix it," Howard said, and turned.

"Burt, I put your stuff in the foreman's room," Shorty Turner told him. "Didn't expect you out tonight or I'da had a fire going."

He led the way, and Howard followed him into what once had been a large bedroom. There was a big double bed in a corner, chairs and a bureau and table, and the floor was covered with a worn carpet. The front door to the living room had opened and he heard Nell's voice.

Howard went into the living room. She looked at him and smiled.

"Welcome to the NC, Burt. I heard you come in. Have you had supper? Very well; come on over to the house and I'll warm up something while I give you the layout here. You're in full charge, Burt. Come along."

He followed her out and the cook stuck his head through the doorway into the living room. "So that's this hardcase Howard, eh?" he sneered. "High an' mighty. An' she's cookin' supper fer him. Well—"

"Well," cut in Shorty's voice with that peculiar lisp

because of his horribly twisted and smashed lips, "you just better let it rest right there, cookie."

Burt Howard walked over with the woman and they entered a low, comfortably furnished home. Its newness told him that it had been built during the four years since Nell Corley had inherited the ranch. It was a tribute to her energy, her fearlessness, her driving ability. They went into the kitchen, where she lit a lamp and placed it on the dining table. He sat down and rolled a cigarette and she went to the still warm oven.

"So you're in the clear?" she asked, bringing out pans and placing them on top.

He told her briefly what had happened. He felt an uneasiness spring up inside of him at sight of her long-legged, lithe body moving about the stove. There was no sitrring there of desire for her, just as there now were nothing but fading memories of what had happened in the past that night of the massacre. He knew that the men would talk, that talk would spread, and that people would begin to whisper that his job as ramrod of the NC was something more than impersonal. Perhaps, he thought, that's just as well. It can make a good cover-up for the job to be done on Broadhurst.

He put aside the thought and began to ask her questions about the ranch.

"How many head?" she repeated, in answer to his question.

"I've got a little over eight hundred head of stockers, most of them with calves for the spring roundup. My bulls are heavy strain, part longhorn and part Hereford. Good hardy strain. There's some odds and ends of stuff left over from the beef sale last fall. Normally I've held the calves for two years up until last fall, when I sold off everything."

"Why?"

She laughed at that one. "Because, Burt, John Broadhurst was putting on the pressure. I thought I'd better pare down to the bone."

"Rustling?" he demanded sharply.

"No signs yet, but I know John too well. He wouldn't let a little thing like stealing cattle stop him from getting what he wanted. You know something?"

"I'm listening," he said shortly.

"I should have married John. With a man like him, who rides roughshod over any obstacle to get what he wants, I could be as tough as hickory and as hard as granite—just as I could be tender with a man I loved. I think I could have made life so miserable for him he'd have been glad to admit he'd made a bad bargain." She laughed at the look on his face. "Don't worry, Burt. Just a thought. I'll have supper ready for you in a minute. Tomorrow morning you take full charge. I'll call up Herbert, the foreman, tonight and make it official, though he already knows it. He may quit or he may appreciate a winter job enough to stay on as straw boss."

"What about the others?"

He had looked them over with a swift, passing glance that had already told him. Middle-aged men who appreciated a winter job; men gone to seed; and men with no fight in them. He thought he could depend upon Jeb. He was pretty sure that Shorty could hold up his end. No matter how much the little rider had been broken in body and spirit under Buck Lake's brutal boot heels, the man still had gratitude. Still, Burt wasn't sure. Shorty might hold up under pressure and he might break again. Burt would have to keep that in mind.

He asked another question: why hadn't Lake whipped the present riders and driven them out?

She brought a bowl of potatoes to the table and put them down. "No fight in them, Burt," she said. "John figures they're harmless, and he doesn't wish to move too fast. There's enough resentment against him already, though people are afraid to say anything out in the open. He's biding his time. I have the feeling, however, that your becoming foreman will change the picture at once. Well, there had to be a showdown sometime, and now that it's coming I'm glad you're in the saddle. Don't let me down, Burt. Break him and

72

I'll repeat the offer the lovely Mrs. Clay made in the hotel dining room: if there's anything I can ever do for you, all you have to do is ask."

Chapter 10

DAVE BELL'S wild horse camp lay some eighty odd miles almost due west of Carterville, where the flat, undulating prairies and mesquite forests had given way to low foothills covered with clumps of cedar, rising to an escarpment and coming out on top of an area some fifteen miles wide. Here the ground was more rocky, the grass sparse, the gullies deeper. But it was here that the wild horse herds held sway in sanctuary above the plain, here the stallions standing up above on watch could see oncoming riders miles before they arrived. The gullies and small ravines and cul-de-sacs were networked with hidden gates and traps into which Bell and his three bearded companions drove the stock, selecting the best and turning loose the "broom tails" and knot-heads" and other stuff not of build and stamina to bring good prices.

The fact that many of these captured horses bore brands made no difference to the man at all, for the section was ideally suited to his purpose, inasmuch as it abutted on the place where three great ranges came together. And Bell knew the ways of the wild stallions. He saw them descend into the lower country to distant horse herds, whip off any stallions in the herd, and return with a new retinue of mares and geldings. Within a matter of weeks these domesticated animals, especially the mares, having known the feel of rope and hackamore, became as wild and far more cunning than the broom tails. Hence Bell kept constant guard to watch for the returning proselytes, and made easy catches of them. From there it was an easy matter to make a hard run of two or three hundred miles across the line into New Mexico Territory, where the animals brought good prices.

In between, he made direct raids on ranch stock and sold them through certain dealers he knew.

It was a lucrative business, and Bell and his men waxed prosperous and content in the big cabin they had built under a red stone bluff not far away from the plateau's main water supply; a big sink three hundred yards long farther along the bluff.

On the afternoon that Burt Howard drove out to take over as foreman of the NC, the man Kansas ascended the trail leading up past the face of the escarpment and came out into the small valley two miles from the sinks. He had covered almost eighty miles in two days of cold riding, but he knew his ground. He saw the smoke wisp above the fireplace's chimney as he approached the big cabin, saw the door open and a man appear. It was Bell himself, a stockily built, dark man of twenty-six. He eyed the newcomer warily, then suddenly relaxed.

"That's better," grinned Kansas, pulling up in front of the door. "Howdy, Dave."

"Hello, Kansas. Back so soon, eh? Light and unsaddle."

Kansas swung down and unsaddled, then removed the pack from the spare horse. He led the animals out to a corral, turned them loose, came back, picked up saddle and the pack containing his bedroll, and carried them inside. "Where's the boys?" he asked.

"Out. Dump the tarp over there in a corner where you can find room. In your old place. I'll have grub ready by the time the boys git in."

"Good. Been eatin' my own trail grub fer two days."

"How's things down below?"

"Bad in the horse business. Might be good some other way. John Broadhurst wants to see you."

"Yeah?"

"That's what he says."

"Why?"

Kansas came back from the corner and warmed his hands at the fireplace. On the hearth was a huge Dutch oven, almost covered with live coals. Bell was cooking hot biscuits for supper.

"I dunno," the visitor said. "I could guess."

He told Bell what had happened in town the past few days. Outside, the wind was rising; the delayed norther was apparently getting under way. Presently three other men came in and nodded to Kansas, who was helping the horse thief with supper. The cracked iron stove in a corner near the fireplace gave off gusts of smoke into the room as the rising wind struck at the pipe sticking through a hole in the wall near the ceiling.

"So he wants me to gun down this Howard?" Bell grunted.

"I didn't say so, Dave. Buck Lake ain't the kind of a man to let him get away with what he has. Howard, I mean. Buck's as hardcase as they come and he's a bad man with a gun, too. So maybe John has something else in mind."

"All right. I'll go down with you in the mornin' and pow-wow with him. The boys can look after the camp till I get back. Not much doing, anyhow, until the weather warms up. Be nice to get a change of grub."

They finished supper and the wind increased until it became almost a gale. It struck gusts down the chimney of both the fireplace and the stove. By the light of a lantern hung from the low ceiling, the four men played poker until nearly midnight. By now the wind had died down again and the night was less cold. Bell went to the door, opened it, and peered out at the sky. "It's sprinkling rain," he said.

It rained that night and most of the next day. Then it turned colder and began to snow.

For three weeks Kansas remained holed up in the cabin while one of the worst winter storms in years swept down across the prairies. It left a white, frozen land and quite a lot of dead cattle. Kansas, sitting snug and warm in the cabin

76

eighty miles from the ranch, chuckled as he thought of the others of the JB iron out in the cold.

But there came a morning when the skies were clear, the snow mostly gone, and the wind stilled. Leading a packhorse apiece, Kansas and Dave Bell set out for the lower country toward Carterville, some eighty odd miles almost due east. They camped that night and then made a very late start the following morning. Kansas wanted to arrive after dark. They worked a leisurely course on the second day and hit Broadhurst's west boundary just in time to camp and eat a cold supper.

At nine o'clock that night, in pitch darkness, they slipped into the silent corral and unsaddled and went toward the ranch house nearly a hundred yards away.

"There's a dim light in the front room, all right," Kansas remarked. "Could be Buck. We'll see."

It was Broadhurst. He sat with his legs outstretched toward the fire, alone, a glass of brandy in one hand, gazing thoughtfully into the flames. He had not cared to leave the light burning. The room was in semi-gloom as the door opened and the two men came in. Broadhurst stirred from his thoughts. He glanced at the letter that lay beside the brandy bottle. It had come that afternoon. It was postmarked Yuma, Arizona Territory, and the enclosed sheet had contained but one word:

DELGADITO

The Little Thin One.

The Little Thin One whose eyes had smoldered with increasing excitement when he had been told of the guns on the stage; guns that meant freedom to raid and fight again.

The Little Thin One who had carried out his part of the bargain, and had killed everyone on the ranch that night to make sure there would be no witnesses.

And now the name had come back to haunt Broadhurst.

77

The ghost of the Apache raider was now in the room, raised by that letter, and perhaps the ghost of somebody else who knew—Wells-Fargo? the Pinkerton men? possibly a man named Burt Howard?

But one thing was certain: what had been a secret was no longer a secret, and the uneasiness half hidden deep in his mind for nearly three years now was drowned by a surge of sudden new fear. He had to act, to find out... or he would have to run again.

"Howdy, John," Kansas said beside the fire now. "You been asleep or something? You look like you've been dreaming or just seen a ghost. Here he is, boss. Dave Bell. Dave, meet John Broadhurst. We were holed up three weeks on account of the storm."

Broadhurst put down the glass and rose, extending a hand. "Glad to meet you, Bell. Had any supper?"

Bell nodded, his hard glance taking in the bigger man, the room, the brandy bottle. Broadhurst saw the glance. "I'll get some more glasses. Pull up a chair. Be back in a minute."

He returned from the cupboard and poured for them. The two men, still chilled, drank in gulps and hunkered closer to the fire.

Broadhurst poured again for the two, returned the bottle to the table, and leaned back. The light from the flames made flickering patterns on the oak beams above and threw grotesque shadows around the dusty window curtains. Broadhurst would tolerate no woman—except Nell Corley—around the place. His housekeeping, what little there was, was performed by a half crippled Mexican flunkey who worked around the ranch doing odd jobs.

"You wanted to see me," Bell said without preamble. "Kansas offered a guess, but that's all. What is it?"

"I want you to kill a man."

"So I gathered. Kansas told me a few things, enough so that I could guess. Why don't this rip-snortin' Buck Lake do it? Accordin' to Kansas, he's a right rough man when he's

78

riled. I don't know because I never worke., this section before."

"I know you didn't. But you were getting ready to. That's why you sent Kansas down this way to work for a few months and look over the horse herds. Sure, I knew it," he went on at Bell's look. "Let it ride. Buck can't handle it because I won't let him. We're fighting a woman and Howard is her foreman. That's why I wanted an outside man for the job. I'll make it worth your while."

"How much?"

"Five hundred."

"Come again, mister," grunted Dave Bell. "Me run from the law for five hundred when I've got a good setup handling horses?"

Broadhurst was unperturbed at the refusal. He said, still looking into he flames of the fireplace, "Five hundred, a hundred a month on my payroll, fifty a month on the woman's payroll, riding under Howard."

"Small change."

"Burt Howard has got nearly nineteen thousand in cash either on him or hid on the ranch some place; money from the sale of a spread he owned in Arizona. Finders keepers."

Bell's interest had quickened, but it didn't show in his unshaved face. "I might never find it."

Broadhurst's voice didn't change or pause as he answered, "It's probably been some time since you've had a woman, living so far in the back country, and you look like a man who would appreciate one. Nell Corley is a beautiful woman; all fire. It's part of the job that you have her, after you kill Howard, and it will be my job to let the people around Carterville know that you had her."

He knew then he had scored, played on Dave Bell's one weak spot. Bell hadn't had a woman in several months because the winter had been too cold to bring in four of them for himself and his men as they often did during the summer. His eyes had quickened with interest.

79

"Maybe you got something there," he admitted. "I could use nineteen thousand. When do you want the job done?"

"When I give the word. You'll go in town first, where you're not known, and hang around a few days. Get shaved and cleaned up in some better clothes. Get a line on the sheriff, Tom Wade. He tries to be honest but he's afraid of us. Inquire about a job...and be choosy until you can go to work for the NC. Don't recognize me on the street. I'll get word to you from time to time what I want done. If you pull it, there's a five hundred bonus."

"And if I don't," Bell grinned with saturnine humor, "there's six feet under."

"You're being paid to take that gamble. And remember: you've never been around this ranch. Nobody but Buck and Kansas here know anything about this."

He stirred in his chair again, picked up the letter, leaned forward and held it to the flames. It burned and he tossed it, and as the ashes settled he could have sworn that they twisted and crumpled into the dark features of Delgadito, The Little Thin One.

Chapter 11

MEANWHILE, Burt Howard had lain through that first night at the ranch, asleep and awake by turns listening to the rain and the wind. He knew they were in for a bad time, that this storm was going to be a tough one. He awoke again and peered out the window to see broad daylight through the window pane, the area between the house and corrals a sea of mud. It was still raining.

He got up and dressed ane went into the kitchen to find it deserted and icy, the ashes from the fire of the night before dead. His lips tightened in anger. Winter jobs were not too plentiful on most ranges, and this bunch, working under a woman owner, seemed to be set for a soft time of it. They could roll out late and come in early in the afternoon. Loaf and eat in the bunkhouse and play cards around a warm stove until nearly midnight.

Burt went up the steps of the steep stairs and into a room. Two of the men snored lustily. Herbert, who had taken his demotion surlily, lay buried beneath the covers, sound asleep. Howard found the cook in the next room.

The cook, too—his name was "Buckeye"—was dead to the world. Howard bent and jerked savagely at the covers, yanking them off onto the floor. Buckeye let out a groan that was half a yell and opened his eyes, shivering.

"Wha—"

"Get breakfast rolling," ordered Howard curtly.

"It's early and it's rainin'. I—"

"If you want to drive that livery rig back to town in this storm today, I'll pay you off," Burt cut in curtly.

He descended the stairs to his room again. All his clothes had been unpacked the night before and were hung in a closet. He took his slicker and put it on and went off the porch into the mud and water, bending his head against the rain slanting down because of the wind. They were in for a bad time of it, he knew. This was going to be a tough one on cattle and horses. It was the ranchman in him thinking now, handling a situation as he would have handled it on his own spread. He went to the sheds and fed the horses, humped up to shelter themselves from the elements. By the time he returned the wind had slacked a bit and the men were up. Buckeye was in the kitchen, cursing the stove and sullen. He had lost some of his month's wages at poker and spent some of it for whiskey and he was broke. He glowered at the stove and went on mixing flapjack batter.

Nell Corley had given Howard a résumé of the situation, drawing out on paper a crude map of her boundaries and where the disputed homesteads lay to the north. The four occupied by riders working for Broadhurst covered a space one mile deep and three miles long on her north boundary. The abandoned one formerly occupied by Shorty Turner was some distance to the south—and far inside her range. She had let Shorty take it up, hoping that others would be encouraged and thus build a wall against Broadhurst's encroachments. But Buck Lake had taken care of that, and Shorty was a man disfigured for life.

The rain slackened a bit, and after breakfast Burt ordered the men into the corrals to begin some repair work. He realized that idle men meant grumbling, lazy men. That much he knew from being around Army posts. Keep them busy and they won't have time to grumble, was the axiom of Army commanders.

By ten o'clock the weather changed. It stopped raining, though the wind was still blowing, presaging snow and a possible freeze that night.

"You men saddle up and get ready to ride," Howard told

them as they stood dry beneath one of the sheds. "The stock will be hunting shelter in the gullies and draws, and those gullies and draws are running water. Good chance for young calves to get themselves drowned. Haze 'em all out and drive them into better shelter."

"In this weather?" protested Herbert. He was thirty-five, sloppily dressed, the protuberance of his belly showing a man inured to laziness. "Now look here, Howard, I know you want to get in good with the boss—"

"You go pack up," Burt cut in coldly. "By the time you're packed I'll have your money for you. I'll pay you an extra five dollars to drive that livery rig back to town. That's where you're going. This morning."

He went up to the house and saw Nell and told her what had happened: that he had fired Herbert. She went to a big drawer of a desk in a small room off the main, big living room and returned with the money. She had asked no questions. She asked one now.

"Where are you going, Burt?"

"Out with the boys. They'll know where most of the stock gathers in this kind of weather. I'm going to take a swing north and look at the boundary."

"You're the foreman. But a word of warning. That north boundary is Broadhurst country."

"So you told me," he said, and left.

"You want me to ride with you?" Shorty Turner asked that morning as they all prepared to leave. Burt had told him where he was going. "I know that country pretty well, since I tried to homestead it. Remember?"

"You show Jeb the ropes. I'll find my way."

He found it, working his way northward and keeping below the swells and hummocks whenever possible. This was partly instinct from years of riding in the Apache country, where you never rode the skyline when it was possible to avoid doing so, and it was partly to keep out of the wind, which was increasing now. The tip of his nose was almost frozen and he repeatedly removed a warm hand from his glove to rub it.

It was an hour or so later when he spotted the rider. The man was going north, too, and Burt recognized him as Luke, one of the three who had been in the Wells-Fargo station and later in the hotel where the fight had occurred. He was on Nell Corley's range and he was driving a calf before him. Apparently he had figured that the weather was too cold for the NC men to be out and had taken advantage of it.

He was slightly to the west and a bit north of Burt. Howard let him go and swung west until he cut the man's trail. He back-tracked, and down below the bank of a cul-de-sac, where the water poured off the prairies into a deep hole, he found the cow. Only one hoof was showing as she lay buried in the pool, but Howard didn't have to see a picture of what had happened. She had been shot and her calf driven off. When the water subsided she would be half buried in sand and probably not be discovered for months.

Burt remounted and took up the trail again. He brought his quarry in sight just as the man drove into Shorty Turner's abandoned homestead. Burt watched as Luke put the calf into a small grain barn and locked the door. Its bawls of loneliness and misery came faintly to the ears of the hidden watcher. Luke unsaddled and went through the mud to the cabin, and presently smoke wisped up from the rusty kitchen stovepipe above the low sod roff of the cabin. Luke, it appeared, had homesteaded and thus moved in further on Nell Corley's range.

The pressure was very much on.

Howard kept under cover and circled to the west, then north. He dropped his horse into a gully where the small trickles of water from the prairies had formed a small stream of brown water and walked the animal toward the distant barn. He came out into mesquites back of the small barn, swung down, tied his horse, removed his slicker and hung it on the saddle horn. Then he made his way to the back of the barn, from inside of which came mournful calf bawls. The animal wanted its mother.

The smoke still wisped from the rusty pipe, and Howard knew that Luke would be hovering over it until the house warmed. Sparks suddenly flew upward and Burt was certain the rustler was poking at the fire. He took his chance and made for the front door. He paused beside it, shook his gun sharply to loosen it in the holster, and then stepped through the doorway into the cabin, closing the door behind him.

Luke straightened, whirled, and then froze at sight of the visitor.

"What're you doin' here?" he whispered.

"I was going to ask you the same thing."

"This is my place. I homesteaded it legal last week. Get off it!"

"It's no go, mister. I saw you driving the calf. I backtracked till I found where you'd shot the cow and dumped her in the hole to be covered with mud and sand. Get your coat on. I'm taking you in town to the sheriff."

He saw the fear, the desperation in the man's eyes, caught the convulsive downward movement of the right hand. He shot swiftly.

Burt Howard sheathed the heavy Colt and moved closer to the fallen rustler. Luke didn't move as Howard impassively felt of his pulse. The rustler was stone dead. Howard straightened and looked about the cabin, saw the man's bedroll in a bunk of dirty straw. He removed the tarp and wrapped Luke's body in it and went to the barn. The calf came out bawling and Burt led his horse to the house. He lashed the dead rustler face down across the saddle, got up behind, and began to haze the calf back in the direction from which it had been driven. The rain had set in again now and it was slow going until he arrived back at the waterhole. The cow's hoofs were not visible now. She had sunk from sight, and so did Luke's body as Burt Howard slid it over into the deep hole.

There was no feeling of regret, no twinge of conscience. After nearly three years, he had become hardened, tempered of all emotion except hatred of John Broadhurst; a cold, implacable hatred fed by the fires of those years.

He mounted again and drove the calf on toward the ranch. He would explain to Nell Corley that it was a dogie. The secret of what had happened to Luke in the cabin would stay locked up behind his lips, to be one more peg of fear driven into the heart of the man he was going to break and then kill.

Chapter 12

HE DROVE his men mercilessly during the three weeks of that storm, and fired two more of them when they grumbled. Jeb and Shorty had come through, working bedraggled cattle into better shelter in weather often close to zero. Now and then he saw Nell Corley on business, unaware, and not caring that Buckeye was washing dishes in the hotel of Broadhurst and spreading stories with significant winks, while, at the same time, trying to "make up" to the pretty Mrs. Clay. Herbert, loafing and playing dominoes in the Prairie, was talking, too. Bedie Wade listened to the rumors and went her way. Mrs. Clay fended off Buckeye's clumsy advances and said she didn't believe a word of it.

Meanwhile, Broadhurst and his riders had not been idle. Day after day, led by Buck Lake and Kansas, they scouted the country for miles. They poked into brush clumps, looked for fresh dirt, explored the water-filled gullies, and dug into snow banks.

They knew what had happened. They had found frozen blood on the floor of the homestead cabin, close by the stove. But they had to have proof that Kansas' pardner was dead, and so far there had been no trace of the body.

The day after Dave Bell and Kansas came down from the wild horse camp, Broadhurst called Lake into the ranch house. The foreman had just returned from another long, cold ride.

"No luck," he grunted again, and took off his mittens to warm his hands by the fire. "We've scoured every foot of ground for a long ways down on her range. If Howard got him, as we figure, he did a good job of hiding the carcass. What now?"

Broadhurst said, "We've got to make him talk."

"Yeah? How?"

"How do you think?" snapped back the other.

He was nervous, frightened. That letter with the single word, *Delgadito*, written in the center of a sheet of paper had taken away sleep. His nights were a series of nightmares in which all the hidden fears came to the surface and made sleep a hideous hell. Nights had become something to be dreaded because when sleep released the pent up fear and uneasiness in him and brought on those hideous dreams, he never woke until the hangman was knotting the noose around his neck and dropping him through the trap. When the rope snapped Broadhurst would jerk convulsively and come awake, to curse and pound at the pillow and roll over again, with the words *Delgadito, Delgadito, Delgadito* beating away at his brain.

He was drinking more heavily now, and the liquor, plus the loss of sleep, had begun to show. He was red-eyed and haggard. He hadn't shaved in three days when Buck came in that afternoon.

"I don't know what to think," the burly foreman said, sitting down close by the fire. "You ain't the kind of a man to let this git under your skin. Men like Luke are a dime a dozen. But the way you're all upset about him being missin', you'd think he was a long lost brother. But you don't have to tell me. It's connected with this Howard. He's got the Indian sign on you, I'm thinking."

Broadhurst shot him a hard glance. "What do you mean 'Indian sign'?" he snapped. "How come you to make that remark?"

It was Lake's turn to look surprised. "I dunno. It just looks that way. Why don't you let us lay out an ambush for him and down him with a rifle? It'd be easy and nobody would ever know what happened to him. Say the word and I'll rig it."

"I don't want him killed yet. I've got to talk to him first. It's important."

He hadn't told Buck that he had to find out for sure if Burt Howard was connected with those events of nearly three years ago; that if the man were killed Broadhurst would never know if it had been Howard or the Wells-Fargo Pinkerton men who had written that one word on a sheet of paper. The fact that they didn't work that way, plus the knowledge that Howard had been in Hatrack, made John Broadhurst certain that Howard knew something about those past events. He had to talk to the man, to burn out of him, if necessary, any information.

Buck Lake said, "So you've got to talk to him first? It's important, huh? That means I was right. He's got the Indian sign on you. Why don't you tell me what it's all about, John? I know you're hidin' something, because you've never spoke of your past since you've been here."

Broadhurst looked at the man and then rolled his glass between the thick, powerful fingers. He trusted Lake, and he knew that if they caught Howard and forced information from him, Buck would probably find out anyhow.

He said, "All right, Buck," and began to talk. He told in detail everything from the beginning, his carefully laid plans, about picking up the gold, covering his trail and buying in at Carterville. He spoke of Hatrack and the fact that Burt Howard had banked money there.

"So I think it fits," he finished slowly. "He knows something. A Wells-Fargo operative wouldn't have written a note like that. Somebody who knows wanted to scare me. So we've got to bait a trap for Howard, you and me. Nobody else. Then we're going to make him talk."

Buck Lake drew back a little from the heat of the flames in the fireplace. "That's more like it."

"That's more like it," John Broadhurst agreed, and

wondered if there could be a double meaning to Buck's words.

Buck might get drunk someday and talk. He might become resentful and talk. He might be badly wounded and talk. Or he might try blackmail.

Broadhurst gazed at the fire through half closed lids. He thought, yes, that's more like it. You had to find out and you did. And the dancer must pay the devil for fiddling. The fiddler's fee. And now you're dancing.

Buck would have to go. The past must be sealed up air-tight.

"I'll figger out something in the next day or so, John," the foreman said, rising to his feet. "She's got a drift fence over west of the place where the boys homesteaded. I've watched Howard riding it. Guess he figgers we might try to cut in. He's out there nearly every couple of days. We could take him into one of the cabins. Well, the weather's warmed up a bit and I think I'll ride into town. None of her outfit has been in lately, so they're about due. Maybe I'd better start hazing ag'in, huh?"

By hazing he meant working over Nell Corley's cowhands who came to town.

"Suit yourself," the rancher said carelessly, and poured himself another brandy. "They're having a Saturday night supper and dance in town."

Lake went out to saddle a fresh horse, grunting a little to himself. Eighty thousand. That had been quite a haul, and Broadhurst was the kind of a man who could have planned and executed it. The kind who would use it to gain still more and let the men who worked for him make it for him. Massacre, huh? And there had been a lone girl on the stage who had lost her life, brutally.

Heaven help the man who had been the cause of that if the law ever caught up with him! Lake grinned and went on toward the corral. The future was suddenly very much brighter.

90

He arrived in town later in the afternoon, unaware that Broadhurst had, in on the spur of the moment, shaved and then come on in. Lake put away his horse and went over to the Prairie. There was the usual number of loafers playing checkers and dominoes, and somebody must have had some in-between-payday money, for there was a poker game in progress at one of the tables.

Joe moved over. "Hello, Buc. Long time no see. Weather, eh? What'll you have?"

"Shot."

He turned and surveyed the room, watching the players in an abstract way, for his mind was filled with roseate dreams. Eighty thousand. Eighty thousand plus a couple of calf crops and the profits from the hotel. Joe placed the bottle and galss on the counter. Just then the door opened and Shorty Turner came in.

Shorty's clothes were no longer ragged nor his boots run down. He looked respectable, and there was nothing of the cringing little down-and-outer of three or four weeks before in his mien as he went up to the bar. Joe wasn't so belligerent this time, either.

"You know it," Shorty said. "Rye."

After downing his drink, Lake turned. He poured himself a second one. He looked at the small puncher must as a mastiff looks at a small terrier.

"Workin' for Nell Corley now, huh?" he asked.

"That's right," Shorty said coolly, and swiveled his hip further away from the bar. "Any objections?"

"Could be. Some gents never learn."

"Some don't," Shorty agreed significantly.

A man had come up from one of the checker tables and moved over. He was dark and lithe and about twenty-six. Bell eyed the two men with lazy contempt in his eyes and sized up the foreman of the JB iron. Lake saw the look and inwardly grinned to himself. This gun-fighting horse thief was a pretty intelligent man. It looked as though Bell were going to make a play in Shorty's behalf to get himself in solid with Nell Corley. Lake decided to encourage him. It would look better after the gun fighter went to work on the NC; widen the breach between the two outfits, clearly establish the antagonism not only between the two ranches but between the two groups of riders.

Lake let his hard eyes play on Shorty Turner's face. "I don't like the NC or anything about it," he sneered. "I stomped your face in once and I'm goin' to do it again. And if you try to throw that gun on me I'll blow you apart."

Dave Bell pushed forward. The room was silent now. "The name is Cole Edwards," he said easily. "I wanted to talk to this little feller here. I'm looking for a job. I heard that this feller Howard, the NC foreman, could use good men. You reckon I could get on?"

"Burt's in town," Shorty replied, obviously relieved at the interruption. He shook hands. "I'm Shorty Turner. You might look him up. But maybe I ought to tell you it ain't supposed to be healthy to work for the NC. You see this face of mine? Buck's done that to three or four of her men. He might try to do it to you."

Dave Bell turned and Lake took the initiative. Shorty was caught off guard at his sudden lunge and went down on the floor under the big man's body. Chairs scraped and the sound was accompanied by the opening of the outer door. The inner, swinging doors pushed in and Burt Howard moved forward as Lake came to his feet to use his bootheels again in Shorty's face. He paused and went rigid. Howard stood with his right hand low at his hip. Shorty got up, picking his weapon from the floor where Lake had slipped it from the holster. He sheathed it. If it had to come, he wanted an even break all around.

Chapter 13

Burt had come into town in the rig with Nell because the ranch was running short of supplies. For three weeks he had driven himself and his men mercilessly and almost to the point of exhaustion while the storm had rained and snowed and finally blown itself out. Not a one of them had been to town in nearly a month. The stock had come through in pretty good shape, all things considered. There was some extra stuff left over from the fall sale, and this he had urged Nell to get rid of. He had advised her to sell stockers, or breeders, along with the calf crop, and turn the ranch into a straight beef outfit; buying stuff from yearlings to two year olds and holding them a year or so before selling for prime beef. It elminated all the trouble of breeder cows growing old, of calf losses, of the nerve-wracking spring, or calf roundup.

To this she had readily acquiesced without hesitation. She was a woman who had been raised on a ranch and knew the business, and her foreman of nearly a month had quickly demonstrated that he was a cowman who knew his business too.

So now they were all in for an afternoon and night in Carterville, leaving only one hand on the ranch. For Burt had gauged Broadhurst well and knew that the man was playing a game too deep to spoil it by anything like a bold raid. He knew that strange riders had been on her range. He had seen the tracks and, since he was from the Apache country, those tracks told a story. Men didn't ride in circles and approach mesquite and cedar clumps when they were hunting cattle. Rustlers didn't work that way.

But the sand had filled in the waterhole well, and there was no trace now of the cow or the man who had shot it. There never would be. They'd ride a long time before they found Luke.

Shorty and Jeb and the two new men—drifters—Burt had hired to replace the men he had fired loped past and went on ahead as Carterville came into view. Nell was sitting close beside him, the cold bringing color to her cheeks. It was Saturday night and there would be a dance in town.

She stirred beside him and said, "Will you be taking in the shindig in town tonight, Burt? They have one every Saturday night during the winter months, except when the weather is bad."

"All depends on a number of things," he answered briefly, and flicked the lines on a flagging rump.

"You mean John and his men? Burt, be careful."

"It's my neck," he answered shortly, and drove on in silence.

He let her off in front of Bedie Wade's small dress establishment and touched his hat brim as he saw her through the window. Nell turned on the porch, her wrapped up dance dress beneath one arm. "See you later, Burt.

She went inside, and he swung the span around in the middle of the street and drove them over to the livery in back of Broadhurst's hotel. A few people lounged in the lobby, but most of them were in the bars, drining and waiting for the festivities to begin. He saw Buckeye over by the stove as he came in, and was unaware that the ex-cook on the ranch had seen the rig as he and Nell drove down the street and had been talking while giving off significant winks and grinning. Howard paid for a room in advance, then walked into the dining room. Mrs. Clay came over to serve him.

"It's good to see you again, Mr. Howard," she said, and he became aware that nearly a month had done wonders for her. The worry and timidity were gone. She was an amazingly pretty woman.

"Just call me Burt," he said. "How's the youngster?"

"Growing like a top, but Dad's spoiling her. And while we're at it, call me Mary, Burt. You shouldn't be eating, though. They're giving a box supper in the dance hall before the dance gets under way. I would tell you how to recognize the one I fixed, so you could bid on it, but it wouldn't be fair to the girls."

"You just tell me," he smiled at her. "I'll bid on it."

She shook her pretty head and laughed. "Buckeye has been bedeviling me for the past week, but I wouldn't eat with that man for all the money in the world." Her face had sobered. "He's the man you fired off the ranch, Burt. He's working here washing dishes. And ... Burt, he's been throwing some pretty broad hints about you and Nell Corley. I just wanted to warn you. I guess I'm about the only one in town who doesn't believe it."

He rose from the table. "Thanks, Mary. If I'm going to buy myself a box supper, there's no use in eating twice. And save a couple of dances for me, will you?"

"I will if, during the tags, you'll cut in on Buckeye every time you see him dancing with me."

"As bad as that?"

"Worse. He tries to court me in the kitchen and even waylays me on the way home to walk with me. The fool has even been gabbling about us getting married. Ugh! As if I could stomach something like that around after the husband I had. He was a ranch foreman ... killed by a stray bullet from a gun fight."

He told her that he'd see her at the dance and went out, strangely disturbed. He had been close to Nell for weeks now, seeing her daily, and now and then catching something in her face she hadn't known was revealed. The hunger and loneliness of a lovely woman for a man. But Mary Clay stirred him as Nell never had. He wondered if it was because of what had happened that day in the Wells-Fargo office, or because of a feeling of pity for her; or was it because Nell had been right when she had said a lovely young widow was far more attractive to men than her unmarried sisters?

He passed through into the lobby and saw Buckeye, who gave him a mocking wave of the hand. Burt nodded curtly, with a brief flick of his head, and opened the door.

He heard Buckeye say, "That's him, boys. Hardcase clean through except when he's around his purty boss, ha, ha!" And more laughter followed, knowing laughter. Up the street, Shorty crossed the intersection and entered the Prairie. Burt remembered the belligerent Joe and followed. He remembered, too, that it was Saturday, that Lake and the other JB men probably would be in town, and he remembered that the fight was out in the open now, that Lake might start his hazing again, beginning with Shorty.

Burt went leisurely up the street. He went in through the outer storm door and in through the swingers just as Lake rose to start stomping in Shorty's already disfigured face. Buck Lake saw him and Burt said, "Don't do it, mister."

He stood with his hand low at his hip and watched the bigger man's right shoulder, waiting for the first downward twitch presaging a flashing grab for the pistol.

"Get your hand away from that gun, Lake, or I'll kill you," he said quietly.

"Maybe," Buck Lake said. "But if you'll pull off that gun I'll show you what happens to gents who hide behind a woman's skirts."

"I don't see any around now. Throw that gun, if you've got guts enough."

A man moved. Dave Bell. He didn't want Lake to do the job he had been hired to dop to spoil the game and ruin Bell's chances for a gamble of nearly nineteen thousand dollars and the pleasure of forcing Nell Corley into his arms.

"Why don't you fellers take it easy?" he drawled. "Shucks, this is Saturday night an' there's a dance comin' up."

Burt saw a darkly handsome face, newly cut hair, shiny boots. He saw bold, flamboyant eyes looking a little amused. He pegged this man as devil-may-care and dangerous.

"You a friend of his?" he asked sharply.

"Nope," was the cheerful reply. "But I know who you are and I don't want to see the man I'm fixing to ask fer a job punching cows getting either shot or put in jail. You gimme a job and I'll even side you against him. The name is Cole Edwards."

"You're hired." And to Lake: "You tell Broadhurst that if any NC man is beat up in town by you or any of his other men, I'll take it as a personal affront and kill the man on sight. Get out, Shorty."

Shorty went out. Burt turned his back on Lake and followed. Dave Bell took off his hat and made an exaggerated show of wiping sweat from his brow. "Whew!" he laughed. "That feller ain't to be monkeyed with."

"Yes?" Lake sneered at him. "Well, since you're workin' for him maybe you'd better get out too."

Bell was aware of the tense spectators. This was good. He'd enjoy throwing a gun against Lake's speed sometime were it not for the fact that they were both working for John Broadhurst.

"Maybe I had," he laughed. "Me . . . I'm a peaceable feller. You do the fighting, mister. My specialty is the ladies. You live longer and have more fun that way. See you fellers at the dance."

He swaggered out, and the storm door banged behind him.

Chapter 14

THE DANCE hall was in a big, square frame building, a former general store whose owner had gone bankrupt from too much credit during lean years. It was some forty or fifty odd feet wide and about one hundred feet long. The floor was smooth, freshly sprinkled with corn meal, and large enough to hold three square dances at the same time. Against the west wall was a low platform with a piano and chairs for the other musicians, whose instruments now were scattered around on top of the piano, the chairs, and the platform floor. At the back a number of abandoned counters had been placed lengthwise, and on them were piled box after box of food, neatly wrapped and done up in ribbons, with the owner's name inside.

These the judge would auction off to the highest bidders, the proceeds from the supper and dance to be used in putting a new roof on the local church. Howard went over shortly after dark, accompanied by Jeb and Shorty. The place was pretty well filled by the time they arrived. Howard saw Judge Burns talking with a group of women down at the lower end and stepped inside. A man's voice said, "Hold it, men."

It was the fat-faced deputy, Bill Stover. He stood just inside the doorway, an open-topped wooden barrel upright on the floor beside him.

"The guns go in here, boys, until you get ready to leave. Guns and dances don't go together here in town."

Burt unshucked his belt and dropped it on top of several others, and Shorty and Jeb followed suit. Feminine laughter came from behind them and Burt turned as Bedie and Nell came in.

"So you got here?" Nell asked, low-voiced, as Burt nodded to Bedie Wade. "We've already heard. It's all over town. Burt, be careful.

"That's what you said this evening coming in," he reminded her and let it go at that.

Nell displayed a box, covered with paper, of the same kind Bedie carried wrapped beneath her arm. "Bedie had plenty of deviled eggs and salad and such left over, and we fixed a box for me."

"Any chance to peek?" Burt asked Bedie Wade.

She shook her head, smiling faintly, and he thought that, oddly, there was worry in her face. He had no way of knowing that word of the new clash between Buck Lake and himself had spread quickly and that the girl was thinking of her father, his fear of an open range war, and the lack of courage he might display at the crucial moment.

The girls passed on down the length of the hall and Tom Wade, who had been with them, beckoned from the doorway. "See you outside a minute, Burt?" he asked.

Howard followed him out into the night. They stepped to the end of the porch, alone.

"Burt, I heard about what happened between you and Buck a little while ago," Wade said. His voice was calm, but Howard sensed the uneasiness back of it. Too bad about Wade. He was straight-forward and he was honest, but he hadn't been cut out for the job of handling the situation now confronting him, which was growing bigger and more ominous every day. "We can't have anything like that take place here."

Burt said coldy, "What did you expect me to do—stand by and let him stomp Shorty's face in again? What would you have done if I had—picked him up and taken him to the doctor or the funeral parlor and then hauled Lake up for a ten-dollar fine levied by Summers?"

Something like a sigh went out of Wade's breast; a tired sigh. "I know. I just don't want it to happen, that's all."

Burt Howard asked a question, his voice a little softer now because he felt sorry for this man. "Tom, you're afraid of them, aren't you?"

That tired sigh again. "I suppose so, Burt. I've tried to fight it down, but I keep remembering what happened to Taylor, the sheriff I succeeded, and how this nick happens to be in one edge of the badge I'm wearing. He tried to do what was right, too. But he didn't have a motherless girl to look after. I have. The only reason I haven't resigned is because everybody in town would know why. I haven't got the nerve. I'd have to pull stakes and leave. Pride won't let me do it."

"What about good deputies?"

A shake of the head. "I'm only allowed two. Bill in there is sort of on pension, like Tobe Summers. Poke Stanton is willing but not of the caliber to stop an outfit like Broadhurst has."

Burt Howard felt sorry for the man. He knew now that Bedie Wade, keeping house for her father, knew only too well the fear in him, and he understood her unsmiling countenance tonight. The thought struck him with the force of a sledgehammer that she might hold him, Nell Corley's foreman, to blame.

"I don't want a clash with Lake or the others if it can be avoided, Tom," he told the sheriff that night on the cold porch. "But fines don't go any more with JB punchers who beat up my men because Broadhurst is putting the pressure on Nell. I told Lake tonight that I'd kill him if he started the haze. If it has to come, I'll try to make it an even enough break to claim self-defense."

"Can you do it?"

"I can try. I'm not a gun fighter. Let's go inside. It's cold out here and they're starting the auction."

They moved into the big building and removed their coats and caps, placing them on a long counter alongside the dance musicians' platform, already piled high with wraps. The crowd had mushroomed toward the lower end of the hall and, amid gibes at his awkwardness, Judge Burns climbed up and stood beside the stacked boxes, looking down at the crowd. Burt saw Lake and Kansas and other men he knew were JB, and he saw Broadhurst, freshly shaven, talking with Nell Corley. He spotted his new man, Cole Edwards, and saw the flamboyant eyes playing with open admiration on Nell's lithe figure. A devil with the women, Howard thought fleetingly, disinterestedly.

"Folks," Judge Burns called, rasing a hand for silence, "here in these beautiful boxes are subtle traps for the unwary—things that put halters on hardened bachelors and turn them into meek and obedient plowhorses. (Much laughter.) Food prepared as only the sly can fix it, opening the path to a man's heart via his stomach. (More laughter.) But the sooner we finish the auction, the sooner we can eat and get on with the dance, and the sooner we can put a new roof on our humble community church. So no more words— let's have some action."

He bent and picked up a former shoebox, now decorated with a flimsy paper wrapping and tied with blue ribbon. He smelled it and gave an exaggerated sigh. "I smell fried chicken. Freshly cooked fried chicken. I can tell by my nose that the two drumsticks are packed here in this corner. (Again the laughter.) Who likes fried chicken? How much am I bid, gentlemen? The loving hands that prepared this might be those of the wife of a very fortunate man, or those of a very lovely maiden. Bid, gentlemen. Bid generously."

The spirited bidding began. Burt remembered that Bedie Wade and Nell Corley had been among the last to arrive and that, therefore, their boxes were near the top. Others appeared to sense it too, for the bidding on that first box was fast and furious. It sold to a young cowpuncher for six dollars, and turned out to have been prepared by the wife of the local minister. Burt turned to Mary Clay, who stood close by. He moved over and looked down.

"Which one?" he asked. "Give me the signal and I'll buy."

"Not unless Buckeye is bidding on it," she whispered back at him. "There he is over there. He's been watching me."

Buckeye, a little drunk already, had been throwing glances her way, watching the expression on her face, and grinning his stupid grin.

The auction proceeded, and when the judge held up a nice-looking box Burt called a bid of five dollars. Somebody raised it to six. Burt bid seven and it was sold. He pushed through the crowd and paid his money and came out, the prize in his hands. He moved over to one of the abandoned counters ranged along the walls and lifted himself up, feet dangling, and began to untie the ribbon. Then he saw Bedie Wade coming toward him, and he didn't have to finish unwrapping to look at the name inside.

"It's my lucky night, Miss Wade," he smiled at her. "Here," putting down the box and sliding to the floor, "let me help you up." He placed his hands under her armpits and lifted her, seating her on the counter, then resumed his seat, removing the outer paper from the box.

The room was filled with laughter, a hubbub of voices; people were spreading out, finding seats to eat with their "pardners." Burt saw Herbert, the paunchy ex-foreman of the NC, eating sullenly with a rolypoly girl all of fifteen, most of whose upper front teeth were missing. Buckeye was guffawing with the wife of the town merchant. Nell sat with the new man he had hired but two hours before. And Mary Clay ate with Judge Burns himself. Broadhurst had not bid. He had grandiosely donated twenty dollars to the fund.

It was long past Burt's regular supper time and he ate ravenously of the food, a little ashamed of himself. He told Bedie so, and her answer came back readily. "I had to sample all that food while fixing it, Burt. It took the edge from my appetite. You eat it."

He sensed the undercurrent of unhappiness flowing

through her like the swift waters of a clear stream flowing over rocks, and he had to know, to bring it to the surface; to find out.

"What is it, Bedie?" he asked her. "Is it Tom?"

"So you know?" she asked, low-voiced.

"I talked with tonight out on the porch."

"He could have handled things until you came along," she said in a matter-of-fact voice. "Nell would have fought alone, and she would have come through somehow. She's that kind of a woman and I love her for it. But you come in here out of nowhere. For some strange reason I won't ask, you're bitter aginst John Broadhurst and his men. You have a grudge against them. I can feel it. It wasn't chance that brought you to Carterville. It was some strong purpose. Oh, I won't ask what it is. You wouldn't tell me and I don't want to know. All I know is that Pop is caught up in the middle of it, and when the time comes for a showdown he's going to break."

"Maybe not," he said, and closed the lid on the box with its scattering of bread and chicken bones and the rest of the residue from what she had prepared. "And you shouldn't hate me for that, Bedie. We all have our destinies to work out in our own way. You, Nell, your father, and myself."

"You could go away. You could go away and let things go on as they were." Again her voice was low, though he sensed the antagonism, the hurt in it. The fear for Tom Wade.

He said, "There go the musicians for the first number, getting ready to tune up. I'll go put this box in the trash barrel by the rear door. I believe it's customary for the bidder of the box to dance the first number with the lady who prepared it. Will you?"

"Of course."

When he came back she was still sitting on the counter. The music broke into a slow waltz and he found her in his arms, his right hand down around her waist, moving smoothly across the floor, the cornmeal sliding smoothly beneath his boot soles. Other faces floated by. The slow

103

waltz droned on and came to a finish, and he claimed Nell for the second dance.

"You're to be complimented," she said, snuggling her body close inside the circle of his arms. "John said you certainly appear to be a competent foreman. He said that Luke had quit the ranch a month ago to homestead on Shorty's old place, and now Luke has disappeared." She pushed back to look up at him. "You killed him, didn't you, Burt?" There was no question in the words. It was a statement of fact.

He felt the muscles of his face tighten and pulled her up closer. It wasn't desire, though he felt it. He wanted to get away from those clear, questioning eyes that were almost accusingly accurate.

"You should have known you'd have to expect such rumors after what happened the first day I came to town, and then went to work for you." His voice was harsh. "You'd better be more concerned about other rumors. Buckeye and the man Herbert have been talking."

"So I heard. It's all over town. Let them gossip, Burt, I fought hard for what I've got and I'll fight harder. I'm above petty gossip. It slides from me like water off a duck's back, because I'm above it. But I won't ask any more questions about Luke. You killed him. I know you did. And you had good reasons for doing it or it wouldn't have happened. You're that kind of a man. Burt, I'm happy tonight. I'm happy because it was the luckiest day of my life when I hired you to ramrod my outfit."

He said, "Maybe. Maybe not."

"I know. You didn't just happen to come here. You came for a purpose. I asked you once, in the hotel dining room, and you didn't answer. I knew then. I'd like to ask you again, but I know you wouldn't tell me. Never mind. Let it go. It's your business, not mine. There's Cole Edwards, that new fellow you hired, dancing with Mary Clay. He looks like a good man."

"If he's not I'll fire him," Burt said, unaware of the harshness in his voice.

"Of course you will, because you're what they call you: hardcase. Hardcase Howard. The name fits you perfectly, Burt."

He was glad when the dance was finished.

The third one was a tag dance and Burt waited on the sidelines. He saw none other than John Broadhurst claim Mary Clay, waitress in his own hotel, for the dance; saw Buckeye, also standing on the sidelines, watching. Buckeye moved forward, threading his way among the couples. He tapped Broadhurst on the shoulder, took Mary in his arms, and felt another tap on his shoulder.

"Tag dance," Burt said.

"But I ain't danced with her yet," the ex-cook half snarled. "Ain't you got manners enough to let us—"

"No manners at all, Buckeye. I claim Mary for the dance."

She already had disengaged herself and moved into Burt's embrace. "Thanks, Burt," she whispered, and he saw her flushed face, prettier than it had ever been before, the color in her cheeks. Maybe Nell had been right. She was the most desirable woman he had ever held in his arms. "That man revolts me. He's after me all the time. I've been thinking of quitting my job and getting another one. I see him a hundred times a day when I go back to the kitchen. Burt, why is it that men take a widow for granted?"

"They don't," he said. "Not all of them. Low mentality and stupidity play a big part in it."

"The fool even tried to grab me and kiss me once. Anything can happen to the mind of a man like that, and I'm a little afraid of him. Burt, what am I going to do?"

"Take a job cooking at the NC. Good food cooked by a woman will make the men work harder, cut the profanity around the place, and Nell needs companionship. It's not right for her to be there alone all the time. Will you take the job?"

"I'd love it. My father and mother can take care of Margaret and I can see her a couple of times a week. And I don't like the way Mr. Broadhurst has been looking at me. He said tonight that maybe I ought to come out to his ranch and cook for him when he's away from town."

"You're working for the NC now," he said.

Chapter 15

AT ELEVEN o'clock the dance broke up for fifteen minutes to give the musicians a brief rest. They had been "breaking it down" for fifteen minutes in a triple square dance. Not once did they pause or falter, not once did the chant of the caller cease.

> *Chase the redbird, chase the squirrel,*
> *Chase that pretty girl 'round the world,*
> *Do-ci-doe, a little more dough, a little more*
>   *dough...*

The dancers swung, do-ci-doed, and "circled in the middle of the floor" while the spectators looked on from the sidelines. The two big stoves in the hall were roaring hot, and the dancers, after fifteen minutes, were beginning to perspire. Finally a big red-faced, puffing rancher let go with a shrill whistle and it was taken up by the other men. The music stopped with a crash. The dancers, panting from exertion, had had enough.

Burt led Nell through the throng, panting, and found that he was laughing with her and the others. It was the first time he had laughed that way in a long time, and the fleeting thought pushed itself into his mind that the past had begun to blot itself out. He remembered, of course, but the ache was no longer there. Nearly three years now.

"I'm going outside and get some fresh air," he said. "It's hot in here. Coming, Jeb?"

Jeb had his arm around Mary's waist; his homely face was all agrin. "Are you crazy?" he snorted. "Me give up the company of a purty girl to go with you? I'm a-stayin' right here, mister."

Burt followed the masculine stream mushrooming toward the front door. Out there they would cool off, talk a bit, and retrieve hidden bottles brought along and left outside. Burt found himself on the end of the porch where he had talked with Tom Wade. The man with him wasn't Wade now. It was Broadhurst. He had moved in.

"Nice dance," he observed.

"Seems that way," Burt agreed, rolling a cigarette before his fingers began to chill.

"How'd Nell come through the storm?"

"Not bad. One cow missing."

"Better than me. One puncher missing. Luke."

"Seems to me you stated he'd quit a month ago and homesteaded Shorty Turner's old place," Howard said coldly.

"Maybe. What happened to him, Howard?"

"I killed him," was the harsh reply.

Broadhurst seemed unpertrurbed at the information. "I know that. We found frozen blood down on the floor by the stove. We couldn't find any tracks because the rain had obliterated them. So you're making war on the JB, eh?"

"I'm making war on cattle rustlers," was the stony answer. "I caught him running off one of Nell's calves. I back-tracked to where he'd shot the mother. I followed him and his tracks to the barn where he hd the calf locked up and went in after him to take him to town and turn him over to Tom. He made the mistake of trying to go for his gun. I shot him."

"Trailed him like an Apache, eh? You said you came from Hatrack. That's Apache country, isn't it? A man tracker."

"I got him."

"What did you do with him?"

"That's what you've been trying to find out for three weeks. You can keep on trying."

"We'll find out. Don't worry about that. And when we do I'll square accounts."

Howard had lit the cigarette, was holding the match cupped in his hands. His eyes and thin nose above the flame threw the harshness, the bleakness of his expression into bold relief. He blew a puff of smoke and it mushroomed toward Broadhurst's face. He didn't reply, because from around the corner where a group of men were talking and laughing and drinking came the voice of Buckeye.

It was loud, important; the kind of tone that told of a circle of entranced listeners. "Yep, you fellers can take that fer the gospel truth. I seen it with my own eyes that night. They was right in front of a window, a-huggin' an' a-kissin' an' not carin' who seen it. Ever' night he'd go up to the house to talk 'business' with her. Ha, ha! You'd think a feller like that would be satisfied with one woman as purty as Nell Corley. But is he? Not by a long shot. He's had his eye on Mary, that gal who works with me down at John's hotel. He knowed she was my girl but that didn't faze him plumb a-tall. So what does he do? Tonight he hired her as a 'cook' out on the NC! Two women he's got now."

Revulsion whipped through Burt Howard. He turned and stepped off the porch and moved toward the group. Buckeye was the center of attraction in a ring that was all ears. He was tilting a quart bottle to his lips, and Burt Howard saw the familiar bulk of Herbert standing by. In spite of the darkness he knew that the ex-foreman was grinning like a gargoyle. The bottle lowered and then Burt had him by the shirt front.

He slashed an open palm blow against Buckeye's cheek and backhanded with another. The bottle fell and made gurgling sounds as Burt forced him back against the wall of the dance hall and slashed him again and again. He flung him to the ground, tensed before he heard the rush of feet. He spun as Herbert, full of whiskey courage, lunged in.

He felt his left hand lift hard and sink into the man's protruding stomach. Pain shot through his right knuckles as he caught the man on the jaw with a looping blow and knocked him down. He was aware that Buck, Lake and Kansas were watching. He could see better in the darkness now.

"Get up," he said tonelessly to Buckeye. "Get up or I'll stomp your face in with a boot heel."

"Now wait a minute, Burt," the ex-cook began, but he didn't finish.

Burt had grabbed him by the shirt front and hauled him up. He slammed the man hard against the side of the dance hall and his back made a thumping sound against the boards.

"Stand there and don't move," he said, "or I'll kill you."

Herbert was trying to get up. Burt gripped him by the shirt front with both hands, because of his heavier bulk, and heaved. He slammed him hard against the wall alongside Buckeye.

Then he stepped back, panting a little. "Now tell them that you lied. Tell them!"

They didn't get a chance, for three men pushed through: Wade, Bill Stover, and a lean-looking man Burt later learned was Poke Stanton.

"All right, boys, break it up," Wade ordered. "There'll be no more of it. You fellows get back inside the hall or we'll jail the whole bunch."

It was over, but Burt Howard knew that night the damage had been done. Word of what Buckeye had said would spread like wildfire, and people would believe because they wanted to believe such things. He didn't care insofar as he himself was concerned. But he didn't want Nell's name mixed up in it.

But Nell's name was already inextricably mixed up in it worse than ever after the dance in Carterville that Saturday night. He sensed it by the looks of the people he met in town. He didn't know whether Bedie Wade believed the gossip or not, but after that night she was more cold and aloof toward

110

him than ever. Broadhurst had spared no pains to spread the news that Burt had admitted killing Luke in a gun fight. It was all over the country by now. And it had put Tom Wade in a bad spot. He was expected to arrest Burt, who was keeping a tight-lipped silence, but there had to be a body produced, and so far both Wade and the JB men had failed. The sheriff and his deputies rode all over the NC range for a week and finally gave it up. They came to the ranch one afternoon and swung down. Burt was in the blacksmith shop shoeing a saddle horse.

"Hello, Tom," the foreman greeted him.

"Howdy, Burt. Well, it looks like you win. Whatever you did with him, he's well hid. We've combed every mile around that section of Nell's north range. Burt, why don't you show us where he is and stand trial on it?"

But Howard shook his head. "There were no witnesses, Tom. It happened just like I told Broadhurst. I caught him with the goods and he went for his gun. The only evidence I'd have is that I drove home the dogie calf whose mother Luke shot. I know it puts you in a bad light, but Broadhurst and his men are after my scalp not only for personal reasons but because I'm siding Nell in this fight." He changed the subject. "How's Bedie?"

"Getting along all right. I guess. Hard to tell about Bedie, Burt. She's pretty deep. I never was able to figure her out, even when she was a tyke."

"I think I have, in a way," Burt replied. "She's worried about you and what you're up against. She hates me because I'm the cause of it."

Wade shot him a queer look. "She don't hate you at all. That's one *I've* been able to figure out."

"Hello, Tom," Nell's voice greeted him from the open doorway of the smithy. "I saw you boys ride in and put on the coffee pot. You must be cold. Come on up to the house and get warm. I've got some cake left."

111

"Nell, why don't you marry me?" the sheriff exclaimed.

"Why, you haven't asked me, you handsome old devil. Come along. Want some coffee, Burt?"

"I just had some," he said. "I'll finish shoeing Red Boy."

He didn't tell her that he'd been in the kitchen with Mary Clay, who was cooking supper for the men still out on the range. He liked her more and more every day, and Jeb Stuart was positively moonstruck over the girl. The bunkhouse was now spick and span, and a surprising number of clean shirts had appeared at the table. The six men of the outfit had become amazingly vigorous with their razors.

But the thought of Bedie Wade plagued him, though he didn't know why. He supposed he was disturbed by the antagonism she felt toward him because of her father. He wanted to make her like him, for there was something in those deep set hazel eyes that affected him strangely.

He put the thought from him and went to work on a hoof with a rasp.

He finished, put the big red gelding into the corral, put out the fire in the forge, and went on toward the bunkhouse. It was getting along toward evening and the others would soon start straggling in.

Mary's little girl came over to meet him as he entered the bunkhouse. He picked her up and held her high over his head and let her dangling legs kick. Mary, in a white apron, came in from the kitchen.

He had the youngster in his lap, listening to her babble about something that had happened at the ranch that day. Nell had insisted that Margaret be brought to the ranch.

"She's crazy about you, Burt," Mary said.

He said, "I'm crazy about her, too. She's my sweetheart."

"It's strange you never married. Never found the right girl, Burt?"

He felt a close affinity to Mary Clay, more so than toward Nell or Bedie Wade. It was because she too had known what it was like to lose someone she loved, suddenly and violently.

112

"Yes, I found her once, Mary. She was killed in an Apache massacre of a stagecoach three years ago while coming West to marry me. Over in Arizona."

"Ah!" There was a new understanding in her eyes. "So that's it? I knew there was something. Nell mentioned it too. She's pretty fond of you, Burt."

"Jeb's pretty fond of you, too, Mary," he answered, and then laughed at the sudden blush on her pretty face.

"Jeb's like all these other womenless men. He's lonesome and hungry for affection. He'd feel the same toward any of a thousand other women."

"Was that what was wrong with Buckeye?" he bedeviled her.

"Oh, him!" She sniffed.

"It must have broken him up real bad," he went on. "So bad that he actually went back to riding. He and Herbert are on Broadhurst's payroll now."

"Good riddance. I—oh, my roast in the oven!" She fled into the kitchen, and Burt sat there with the child in his lap, thinking.

Chapter 16

THE SEVERE winter brought on an early spell of warm weather in March, and one afternoon Dave Bell, riding the drift fence, saw Kansas and Buck Lake and Broadhurst. He put spurs to his horse and loped toward them a quarter of a mile away. They were down on foot, Lake and Kansas busy with wire cutters.

Bell pulled up and grinned.

"Howdy, boys. Ain't you got anything else to do?"

Broadhurst ignored the jest. He was dressed in range clothes and wore a pistol at one hip. He had been spending much of his time on the ranch of late.

"What's new on the NC?" he inquired.

Bell lifted a leg to lock it around the saddle horn and rolled a smoke. "Nothing at all. Howard's gittin' ready for the spring roundup in a couple of weeks. Good thing you boys haven't tried any rustling. He watches this range like a hawk."

"You go back and tell him you found the fence cut," Broadhurst directed. "I want to talk to him private."

"Baiting a trap, eh? Maybe he'll report to the sheriff."

"Wade is set on getting proof. Our horse tracks come in from *her* side of the fence. If he sends out one of you men to repair the damage, then we'll have to try something else. How are you making out with Nell?"

Bell grinned and winked significantly. "I'm makin' out all right."

114

"Just be sure Howard don't figger you're moving in on his range," Buck Lake jeered.

"I think that's one reason she's cottoning up to me like she is," the gun fighter replied. "He don't pay her no more attention than like she was a hoss in the corral, an' Nell ain't used to that. I think she's usin' me to make him jealous. But it ain't workin' and I'm satisfied." He laughed.

"Must be something wrong with him if he don't go after that. A purty woman and a ranch, too." Kansas observed.

Bell said, "I think I know the answer to that one, too. He's a purty closed mouthed cuss except with Mary Clay, that good lookin' little widow cookin' for us. He told her one day he'd lost his girl in an Apache raid over in Arizona about three years agao. Around some place called Hatrack. Seems she was comin' West to marry him an' was on this stage when a bunch of reddies waylaid it at a ranch and massacred the whole bunch, includin' the girl Howard was goin' to marry. So maybe he ain't got over her yet...."

He was talking to Kansas and Buck, unaware that the words had sent a numbing shock of fear through John Broadhurst. The big man stood there, his face impassive, a cold hand having clutched at his vitals. There wasn't any doubt about it now.

That girl on the stage, the one he'd helped on, knowing she was going to her death. Somehow, some way there had been a slip-up. *Howard knew!* Howard was after him. He had trailed him a thousand miles and found him, and for three months this harsh-faced man tracker had been biding his time. Broadhurst understood now a hundred little things he had been puzzled about before. It all came clear in a flash. That letter with Delgadito's name written on a single piece of paper. The mention of Hatrack in the courtroom of Tobe Summers that day. Howard had been baiting him, goading him, forcing those sleepless nights of worry on him... and biding his time.

In that moment the near-panic that seized Broadhurst

115

made him forget all about Nell Corley. He saw Buck Lake looking at him with amazement on his face. Buck knew, too.

"Let's get out of here," he said harshly. "Dave, you go on back to the ranch and tell Howard about the fence. I'll be watching here tomorrow morning, me and Buck. Kansas, you go over to Slim's homestead and tell him to look at the fence around the Red Gap waterhole first thing in the morning."

That was an excuse to get Kansas out of the way. Broadhurst rode with Lake, straight toward the home ranch four miles north and not caring about tracks now.

"So he found you, eh, John?" Lake finally asked.

Broadhurst nodded. "The biggest mistake he ever made. We've got to work fast, Buck. And I feel better now that I know it's him and not Wells-Fargo. I don't know how he got on my trail, but this is a showdown. I can't wait for Dave now. We'll have to get Howard off guard, make him talk, and then kill him and put him away the same as he did to Luke."

"I git the hunch," Lake grinned, "that Dave is more interested in Nell than he is in downin' Howard. I've had that hunch fer quite some time; and a man's no good fer that kind of a job when he's got a woman on his mind. Not only that, but he said he'd searched Howard's room a dozen times and ain't found a trace of that money yet. Maybe he'll have it on him when we catch him, eh?"

Broadhurst grunted.

"And that means I get it for doin' Dave's job, eh?"

"I'll be in on it," Broadhurst said shortly.

Lake eyed him coolly. "No you won't, John. I know too much and you got too much to lose to quibble over dinero. That poke is mine. We'll git him and I'll stomp his face in till he tells me where it's hid. Then I'll go after it."

As for Bell, he rode on toward the ranch, thinking hard. He had told them that Nell might be letting him play up to her because of Howard's seeming indifference. But he was a

116

handsome man and a bold one with the women, and time was growing short. He hadn't found the money, he had lost interest in killing Howard, he only wanted Nell.

"Danged if I don't think I'm in love with her," he chuckled, and took pleasure in the thought. "Why, I could turn respectable down here and still run the layout on the mesa. I could rustle Broadhurst clean. Five hundred to kill a hardcase and get a girl when I can maybe have her and the whole layout to boot. Huh."

He rode on, pleased with the thought. From now on he was going to be the devoted lover.

He rode in and unsaddled. The horse drank from the windmill trough and then went over for a roll while Bell hung his saddle and bridle on a peg beneath the shed. His spurs made clanking sounds as he crossed the porch and entered the living room. Jeb and Shorty looked up and nodded a greeting. Although Bell was accepted as one of the outfit, there was no friendliness on either side. They knew he was "making up" to Nell Corley, that he made almost nightly trips over to the bigger house evenings after supper to play cards with her and talk. That, of course, was his business. But they were riled by his bold attitude toward her and all women, his way of tucking Mary beneath the chin and telling her she was sweet, his arrogance, his don't-give-a-hoot-about-this-job attitude.

He unslung his gunbelt and looked at Burt Howard. The other men hadn't come in yet.

"There's about fifty yards of the north drift fence cut and the wires pulled down," he said casually to this man he was trying to send to his death. "Hoss tracks of three men coming from our side of the range. Thought I ought to tell you."

"Any cow tracks?" Jeb demanded instantly.

Bell shook his head, reaching to hang the belt on a nail. "No rustling. Anybody'd be a fool to try it in broad daylight like that with the track easy to foller. I was there about an hour ago. It hadn't been done long."

117

"All right," Burt said. "I'll take the rig in town in the morning and get a couple of spools of wire. We're completely out anyhow. I'll be back by noon. Jeb, right after dinner tomorrow, you and Shorty take a rig and go up and fix it. Don't look for any trouble. I'll tell Tom Wade, though I expect they've covered their trail."

He rose and went up to the ranch house. Nell was cooking her own supper. She and Mary ate alone after Mary had finished serving in the bunkhouse. He picked up Margaret, who was walking around the kitchen, and hugged her, looking at Nell.

"I'll be going in town in the morning for a couple of spools of wire," he said. "Cole said the north drift fence has been cut. Anything you need from town?"

She came over to him and looked up. "So it's begun in earnest?" she asked.

He nodded and put down the child, giving Margaret a pat on the head. "It had to come sometime. I'll tell Tom, of course. I don't want to. He feels so helpless. I feel sorry for Tom, Nell."

"What about Bedie?" she asked.

"Well, what about her?" he said roughly.

"Still the hardcase, aren't you, Burt? I'll go in with you in the morning. Bedie's been promising for weeks to come out and spend the week-end. She and Tom can stay over while he's looking around."

"In that case, suppose that you go on in alone. No need for me to be away from the ranch. I've got plenty of work to do."

Her eyes were mocking, tantalizing. "Afraid of what people will say, Burt?"

"You know better than that," he said harshly. "I don't give a hoot." She was standing close to him now and he didn't like it.

"You're different from Cole, Burt."

"What Cole does is his business as long as he does his work."

"You don't like him, do you? You and the other boys?"

"No," he said shortly. "Jeb swears he's seen him some other place and his name isn't Cole Edwards. But that's his business too. Bring out two spools of wire. We've got plenty of staples."

He left her, a little angry; she seemed to have a way of making him angry when she was in a devilish mood. Mary, wise in the ways of women, had hinted to him that Nell Corley liked him far more than she cared to admit. He had replied that it was because he was getting things done as foreman. Mary's answer to that one had been a knowing smile and the observation that Cole Edwards was a handsome man.

Howard went back to the bunkhouse. He ate in silence and went to his room. He noticed for the third time that sometime since last night his things had been ransacked. Edwards or the two new men were hunting money.

Chapter 17

HE WENT out to the blacksmith shop and dug down into a pile of dead ashes near the forge and soon uncovered a small lard pail. In the darkness he removed the money belt and put it around his waist. By the time he got back Mary had cleared the table and gone to the ranch house, and the nightly poker game for pennies was under way. It was five-handed stud, and Burt seated himself across from Cole Edwards, or the man who called himself such. He pulled out two or three dollars in change and within half an hour had lost it.

"Looks like it's your off night, podnuh," chuckled Jeb Stuart, raking in a dollar-and-forty-cent pot.

"Looks that way," Burt agreed, and unbuttoned his shirt front. He indifferently removed a sheath of goldbacks in hundred dollar denominations until he found a ten. He was baiting a trap to catch a thief.

"Lordamighty!" gasped out Buster, one of the drifters who had been hired, his eyes bulging. "What did you do— stick up a bank?"

"A stagecoach." Burt grinned, and replaced the money.

"You wouldn't ketch *me* packin' thet kind of dinero around. I couldn't sleep a wink. Fust thing I'd do would be to git me a tomato can an' a post hole digger and bury her deep."

Burt shrugged. "Maybe because I'm honest I figure everybody else is, Buster. It's safer hid in my room than in some banks I could name. But maybe I hadn't ought to leave it around. I'm going in town in the morning for some new wire and I expect I'll put it in the bank."

120

"Believe me, I'd sleep with a six-shooter under my piller with all that money," put in Tony, Buster's pardner.

"I do." Burt grinned and buttoned his shirt.

He went on with the game, and by eight-thirty had cleaned them out of small change. He rose, yawning. "Reckon I'll turn in, boys. Hard day tomorrow."

"That goes for me, too," Bell said, and rose too, pushing back his chair. He took his gunbelt from the nail and carried it up the stairs, and the others soon followed. There were the usual thumping sounds as pulled off boots fell to the floors of the rooms, the gibes and laughter as shivering men jerked off pants and jumped in between the cold blankets, and presently quiet settled over the house except for gentle snores. Bell waited another half-hour, then threw back the covers and rose, fully dressed. He didn't care about Broadhurst now. He knew where the money was, at last, and that was all he had been waiting for. As for Nell, his notion of the afternoon about marrying her had been nothing but idle daydreaming. He and Buck Lake had big plans for the future, and they didn't include Nell.

He strapped on his gunbelt, put on coat and cap, and picked up his boots. The door creaked slightly as he opened it and went out. He avoided the second step because it creaked and made his way noiselessly to the living room, now in darkness. A pale quarter moon showed the outlines of Burt Howard's door, and the gun fighter carefully lowered his boots to the floor and slid a long knife from its sheath. With the weapon gripped in one hand, he opened the door with the other. Through the crack he saw Howard beneath the covers, and smiled. It was cold and the foreman was snuggled down deep. Bell opened the door wider. It was but a single step to the side of the bed and the took it, the knife lifted high in his hand. It slashed down hard through the covers, and from across the room a match flared. In the light of it Bell saw Burt Howard and the .45 Colts six-shooter in his right hand, the muzzle lined at Bell's belly.

121

"Don't move or make a sound," Burt said, low-voiced. "I don't want to wake up the other boys."

He leaned forward and lit the wick of a lamp whose globe already had been removed and then replaced it. The light flared bright.

"What now?" sneered the gun fighter. He weighed his chances, decided against them, and waited.

"The money has been hid under the forge in the blacksmith shop. But I was tired of my room being ransacked. So I baited a trap tonight."

"That ain't the only trap that can be baited," sneered back the gun fighter. "I asked you what now?"

"I'm kicking you off the ranch. You can come back for your pay later. Put on your boots and let's go down while you saddle your horse. You're pulling out tonight."

"Fine. I was gittin tired workin' fer a two-bit outfit, even if the wimmin end of it wasn't so bad. I had my fun with her."

"Get going."

Bell grunted and went out into the living room. He slipped on his boots; his gun was now in Burt's hand. They went to the corral, where Bell saddled and bridled his horse. He swung up and looked down. "Don't I git my gun back?" he asked mockingly.

It came up to him, barrel first, Burt's own gun covering him the while. Bell carefully slid it in the sheath and grinned. There was a light in the living room of the ranch house.

"I'll go over and tell Nell good-bye," he grinned. "She's purty fond of me. I reckon she'll be all upset when I tell her I'm pullin' stakes."

"Suit yourself," Howard said coldly.

Bell said, "Be seein' you, mister," and rode toward the ranch house. He saw Howard enter the bunkhouse and waited until the light in his room went out. Bell grinned and swung down. He crossed the porch and opened the door into the warmth of the living room, where Nell had undressed before the fire. She was in a white gown and wore furry

122

slippers on her feet.

She rose and turned. "Cole, it's not nice to enter a house while a lady is preparing for bed. I saw the lights go out in the bunkhouse nearly an hour ago. I thought you were all in bed."

"Not me. I'm pulling stakes. Burt fired me."

"Oh. And you came for your pay. Of course."

He had moved in closer. He said, "Yes, I came for my pay. And to tell you good-bye."

He had her in his arms, her gasp of surprise telling him that it was unexpected. He felt her tense and push back.

"Cole, cut it out! You're acting like a child. Let go of me!"

He laughed and fought for her lips and crushed her to him. "You never fooled me fer a minute, Nell. You was cottoning up to me to make Howard jealous, and you thought I didn't know. But women don't play that way with Dave Bell. I—ouch, you she-cat!"

He felt the fiery streak across his cheek where her nails had raked him and he slapped her brutally. He heard the scream and his hand clapped itself brutally across her mouth, shutting off all sound. He laughed as she fought him and then began forcing her, half carrying her toward the door. Behind him came a sound and the door he had entered crashed open. Bell spun and saw Howard.

"So you were waiting," the gun fighter sneered.

"I was," was the quiet reply.

"You know who I am?"

"Yes, a dirty coyote I never trusted."

"I'm more than that. I'm Dave Bell. I work for Broadhurst."

Nell had swung to one side out of line of the two tense men. She saw the mockery in Bell's eyes—Dave Bell, the notorious horse thief and gun fighter. She felt sick inside as she thought of herself allowing this man to come into the house evenings.

She saw the paleness, the wariness in Burt Howard's face,

the wall of cold implacableness she had never been able to break through. That woman who had died on the stage.... Mary had told her.

"So you're working for Broadhurst?" Burt asked tonelessly.

"Sure," grinned Bell. "He hired me to put you down when he gave the word. Seems he told Buck Lake about some suspicions he had concerning a massacre over in Arizona two, three year back in which yore girl got killed. But me and Buck are pards now. He's coming into my outfit when we squeeze Broadhurst dry. That fence that was cut this afternoon was cut by Buck and Kansas and John himself. I watched 'em do it. It's a trap to draw you out so's John and Buck can get hold of you and make you talk. He wants to find out how much you know. My part of the bargain was to git a thousand fer the job of downin' you when he give the word, plus that roll you carry, plus takin' Nell fer my woman so's John could spread the word around and drive her off her ranch. But you kinda busted up things by buttin' in here, mister. People don't bust in on Dave Bell when he's with a woman. So I'm tellin' you this because it's outs fer you and I'll take her anyhow."

He drew with lightning speed, his hand flashing beneath the open coat to his hip. A red flash lit the room, turning into a brief orange glow mingling with the light of the kerosene lamp. It came again, and the shock of the two .45 slugs knocked Bell half around and then down. He fell curled up, the gun that barely had cleared the sheath lying close by his fingers. The fingers were curling and uncurling.

Burt stepped forward with the big six-shooter low at his hip, eyes on the figure of the gun fighter laying on his right side. He straightened and sheathed the Colt.

"He's dead," he said. "Are you all right?"

"I'm all right... now," she answered, and suddenly she was in his arms, holding him tightly. He felt the trembling of her body.

124

"Burt, Burt," she whispered. "It was all my fault. I led him on because you wouldn't—oh, never mind. Hold me close. Burt, forgive me."

He didn't hold her close; it was she who held him. He pushed back, and she saw his stony face and knew she had made a mistake.

He turned and saw Mary in the doorway. "Burt . . . Nell, what happened?" she asked.

He told her in brief words. From out in the night came the pad of running feet, men in their socks, and Shorty and Jeb and the others burst into the room. They wore pants and undershirts.

"Holy smokes!" Jeb blurted out. "It's Cole. You got him."

"It's not Cole," Burt Howard said. "His name is Dave Bell."

"Bell! Now I know where I've seen him. Bell! I saw him New Mexico last summer with a bunch of hosses. I know I'd seen him some place before. Dave Bell, that hoss thief gun fighter . . . and you got him."

"Shorty," Burt said. "Bell's horse is saddled up outside. You get dressed and burn the breeze in town after Tom Wade." He sketched briefly what had happened. "And," he finished, "this throws Broadhurst out into the open. He'll hang for plotting that massacre. So keep out of the saloons in case he's up late. Don't say anything to anybody. Just go to Tom's house and tell him."

"I'll git dressed right away, Burt."

Shorty went out into the night again, running, and presently hoof beats drummed off into the night. The men had removed Bells' body, leaving the ugly red splotch on the carpet where the gun fighter had fallen.

Burt went down to the bunkhouse and fired up the stove and put on coffee.

Chapter 18

IN CARTERVILLE that night Bedie Wade sat before the fire in the comfortable living room, reading a book. She was reading aloud to her father, as was customary nearly ever night. Wade sat back in the chair and with half closed eyes watched the flicker of light from the fireplace play over her face. She was much as her mother had been when he had first married, except that there was an undercurrent of reticence in Bedie, a world in which she lived alone.

His eyes went back to the fire as he listened and his thoughts fell away from the story and turned to the trouble brewing. It was coming, it had been coming since the first day Burt Howard had come to Carterville. There was going to be a showdown, a test of men pitting strength and skill and gun speed against each other. And in the midst of it the test was coming for him. Had it not been for Bedie he would have resigned and left to take up life anew where the fear that gnawed at him would not be known.

Nobody but Tom Wade knew that, like Broadhurst, his nights were filled with dreams in which he faced the inevitable ... and always came out cringing, backing down, or going down before Broadhurst's guns.

"Pop," Bedie's voice said chidingly, "you're not listening. I've read most of tonight's chapter and you haven't heard half of it. Getting sleepy?"

"A little."

"Worried?"

126

"Nothing to be worried about, Hon. The jail is empty and the county quiet. I'm just a loafer earning my pay."

She closed the book and put it aside. The firelight made those flickering shadows on her face again. She said, "Yes, but we know that it won't be quiet for long. It's coming, isn't it, Pop?"

"You mean that showdown between Burt and John Broadhurst? Yes, it's coming, pet. I wish I knew what was back of Burt's mind. But he's like you, Bedie—he keeps his thoughts to himself. It's too bad you hate him like you do."

It was a indirect needle and it got the desired results. "Why, Pop, I don't hate him," she denied a little indignantly, and he saw the faint blush of embarrassment on her face. He knew then that the shot in the dark had probed the right spot, opened it wide for a brief moment, and revealed what lay hidden inside.

"No," he said softly, "you don't hate him at all. That's one time I caught you off guard. He's worth fighting for, Bedie."

"I don't understand a word of what you're talking about!" she exclaimed, the color coming to her face again, and rose to her feet.

"It's all right, Hon," he chuckled. "I won't reveal your secret. But there's those reports about him and Nell."

"There's also those reports about her and Cole Edwards. And I don't believe a word of either."

"Neither do I... but you don't have to snap your old man's head off. Burt's got too much on his mind, whatever it is, to have any time for a woman, even one as pretty as you or Nell or Mary Clay. Maybe one of these days he won't have it on his mind any more and then—"

"And then," she cut in indignantly, "I'm going to bed right now. Of all the nonsense I ever heard in my life—"

She paused and Wade came out of his chair. The hoofbeats had stopped in front of the yard gate. They heard the creak of the hinge Wade had been promising to oil for the past month and boot heels on the walk, coming toward the

127

porch. The knock rattled the door. "Come in," Wade called. "Oh, hello, Shorty. How's it going?"

"Cold," the disfigured little man said, moving in toward the fire and taking off his gloves to warm his hands at the fire. "I nearly friz comin' in from the ranch. This is supposed to be early spring, but you wouldn't think so ridin' five miles at night."

"Anything up?"

Shorty straightened and nodded, his horribly beaten face solemn. "Quite a lot, Tom. You know that Cole Edwards feller that's been workin' on the ranch and playin' up to Nell? Well, the way it turned out his name wasn't Cole Edwards at all. It's Dave Bell."

Wade had gone for the decanter of whiskey in the cupboard. He got it and came back with a glass. Something had broken, the first crack, warning of the crash that was coming. He sensed it and he felt fear rise up in him again.

He poured and handed the glass to Shorty, who took the generous slug at a gulp. He sighed and wiped his lips with a sleeve. "Thanks, Tom, that sure warms a feller better than any fire."

"You said Dave Bell. That gun fighter horse thief from over in the mesa country?"

Shorty Turner nodded. "That's right. It was Bell himself, sure 'nough."

"You said *was*," Bedie put in quickly. "What happened?"

"It's *was* all right, Bedie. Dave Bell is dead. Burt killed him in a gun fight at the ranch tonight over Nell Corley."

Wade shot a look at his daughter, but her face told him nothing. Little Poker Face, he thought. In love with a man who had killed another over a woman with whose name he had been linked by gossip.

Shorty went on. "Burt's room had been ransacked several times lately by some gent lookin' fer that wad of money he's got. So tonight he opens the belt in a poker game to let the boys see it an' then says he's goin' to come in town in the

128

mornin' to git some wire—our drift fence was cut by Broadhurst this evening—and as how he'd better bank the money. Cole—this Dave Bell musta figgered it would be his last chance to git the money, an' he fell right into the trap Burt laid fer him. After we went to bed this Bell slipped downstairs in his sock feet an' drove a knife into what he thought was Burt asleep in his bed. Only it was a bunch of quilts. Burt was waitin' with a gun in his hand. He got the drop on Bell, made him saddle up, and then told him to git off the ranch. Cole went up to the house to tell Nell good-bye, an' I guess—beggin' your pardon, Bedie—that he figgered to take his pay another way besides cash. Burt had figgered that one out, too. When he heard Nell scream he busted in and found 'em strugglin'. He told Burt that he was goin' to kill him. He said that Broadhurst had hired him to do the job. Seems as though when Burt's girl got killed in that Indian massacre three year ago, it was Broadhurst who planned the job to git the gold off the stage. Burt had trailed him fer three years, an' John had found out about it an' why he come to Carterville. That fence they cut was a trap laid to git Burt into a' ambush where they could make him talk. Bell told Burt an' Nell all this an' then went fer his gun. Burt shot him twice and told me to burn the breeze in here to git you."

Wade put the decanter of whiskey back in the cupboard. He wanted to take a drink—a big double slug to help give him courage for the job he had to do. He didn't take it because Bedie would know.

He said, "All right, Shorty. You go on back to the ranch and tell Burt and Nell I'll be out in the morning. Nothing I can do tonight. Bell's dead and Burt won't run."

He went over to the wall and took down his gunbelt.

"You ain't comin' out with me?" demanded Shorty.

"No," Tom Wade said. "I'm going out to the Vinegar-roon."

"Pop, take Poke and Bill with you," Bedie said. "Pop, don't go out there alone."

"If John resists arrest, Poke and Bill will only get themselves killed, pet. If he doesn't, I won't need them."

He put on his cap and coat and gloves and went over and kissed his daughter. "Now don't do any worrying. I'll be back in a few hours."

He went out the back door of the kitchen to the small shed and corral where he kept two head of saddle horses. In the silence of the living room, Bedie looked at Shorty.

"Shorty, they'll kill him," she said.

He nodded. "I reckon they will, Bedie, but there's nothing I can do."

He turned to go, and she said, "Wait. Wait until Pop leaves. Then I'll saddle up and go back with you. Nell needs me, and I think that I need her."

Bedie dressed hurriedly in a split leather riding skirt and pulled on her boots while Shorty waited. From out back of the house the sound of trotting hoofbeats finally faded away in the cold night air, and she brought her saddle and bridle from the bedroom. They went out, and Shorty quickly caught and cinched up her mount. He got his own and swung up and they loped westward to cover the five miles to Nell's NC spread. It didn't take them too long, for the night was cold and the horses eager to keep warm. She swung down in front of the ranch house while Shorty led her mount to the corral to unsaddle it. The light was still on in the living room, and Nell met her at the door. Bedie saw that a heavy blanket lay on the floor. That would cover the spot where Dave Bell had fallen under Howard's gun.

"Darling, I'm glad you came," Nell greeted her. "This has been a terrible night. I suppose Shorty told you. Where's Tom?"

Bedie said, "Hello, Mary," and then turned to Nell. "He didn't come."

"He *what?*"

"He went to the Vinegarroon to arrest John Broadhurst, Nell."

"But they'll kill him," Nell cried out.

"I know. But you know Pop. He was scared, of course. I know he was scared. But when he makes up his mind it's made up."

"So's mine. Come on with me down to the bunkhouse."

The three of them went through the night toward the light in the living room of the former ranch house. They went inside to where sleepless men sat around talking in subdued voices. Over in a corner was a long object wrapped in a tarp.

"Where's Burt?" Nell asked. "Where's Jeb?"

"Burt went down to the corral a little while ago and didn't come back," Buster said. "Don't know where Jeb is. He was here a little while ago."

Chapter 19

THEY HAD convincted John Broadhurst after days of testimony in which the whole story of the massacre came out. Delgadito had been brought from Arizona in chains and, speaking fluent English now, told from the witness stand what had occurred. Broadhurst saw Nell laughing at him, this new bright-eyed Nell who always stayed so close to Burt Howard, and he saw the looks on the faces of the jurors as they filed in to render the verdict. When sentence was pronounced pandemonium broke loose in the courtroom. There was a rush of men and he found himself being half carried, half pushed out into the area between the courthouse and jail where a new scaffold had been erected. Pushing hands started him up the steps, all thirteen of them, and he stumbled and fell as they thrust the rope around his neck....

He awoke in the cold darkness of the room as he had awakened so many times before, cold sweat on his brow. He grunted angrily and snuggled deeper beneath the covers. Tomorrow the traps...

The sound came again, his footsteps stumbling on those scaffold steps. It came from the front door. He listened for the sound of Buck Lake's snoring, for Buck had been sleeping in the ranch house of late. Broadhurst was taking no chances on Buck talking with the men and getting a loose tongue.

The rancher rose and slid the six-shooter from beneath his pillow. He put on a robe and descended the stairs in bare feet, moving soundlessly across the carpeting. The knock had come again. He said, "In a minute," and opened the door. The banked fire in the fireplace didn't throw off much light, but enough so that he saw Burt Howard, felt the gun knocked from his hand.

"Step back," Burt ordered. "Don't make a move or I'll blow out your gizzard."

Broadhurst stepped back. He moved over toward the fireplace and Burt lit a match to the lamp. He turned, and Broadhurst saw what was in his face.

Burt said, "Dave Bell talked a lot before he died."

That was all he said, and Broadhurst didn't answer. It had come, and as Broadhurst was prodded across the room to the still warm fireplace, he hoped that a God he had long since forsaken would wake up Buck Lake. For there was no doubt in the rancher's mind as to why this hardcase had come or what he intended to do. He bent and picked up the poker to uncover a glowing mass of live coals, and his hopes faded as Howard stepped back to be free of the deadly blow that did not come.

"Anybody else in the house?" snapped Howard.

"No. I never wanted but one person it it, and I don't want her now after you and maybe Bell have had her."

"I'm not interested in what you think," was the reply. "You won't be after tonight. It will be three years the tenth of next month since the day you let her go out on that stage, knowing she was going to her death in a raid that you plotted."

Broadhurst said a little tiredly, "There's some liquor in the cupboard. A drink will warm us up. I'll get it."

"You stay right where you are," Burt ordered. "I'll get it."

He brought back the bottle and glasses and put them on a table, and the rancher poured. His big face was impassive. He felt his hands tremble and knocked a glass to the floor. It made a rattling sound.

"Well, here's luck," he said, after picking it up and refilling it. "How did you find out?"

The fire was blazing up a bit now and threw light into the room. Burt kept his distance from the man and laid down the gun. Broadhurst was sitting in his favorite chair.

"A hunch at first. Just a hunch that something was wrong. Those Indians who broke off the reservation had good guns, yet none were reported stolen. So they had been furnished. The gold made it look like a white man might have been involved. I back-tracked up and down the line for months and checked every Wells-Fargo man. You were the only one whose background was a blank wall. So it was a matter of waiting and waiting until Delgadito was caught. Did you hear about it?"

"I'm not much of a hand for reading the papers. So they caught him?"

Burt nodded. "Last winter. I talked to him in Yuma prison through an interpreter, an old Indian fighter. It was Al who mailed that letter with Delgadito's name on it, according to my instructions. But the Indian couldn't tell me too much, except that it was a big man who talked his language and planned it for them. I covered every Army post in Arizona Territory asking about a big man who spoke Apache, but it was no go. So I hit for your home country among the Mescaleros in New Mexico. When I asked an Army colonel he said that sounded like Broadhurst, and I knew I'd hit the jackpot. But the trail was two and a half years old and you could be anywhere. I played a hunch you'd have used the eighty thousand in gold to start ranching, and wrote to the capitals of Arizona, New Mexico, and Texas. Austin said there was a JB iron registered to John Broadhurst, at Carterville. I came in, and the moment I saw you in the hotel that night you sicked Buck Lake and the others on me—I knew in that moment, from the Army colonel's description, that I'd tracked you down."

His voice was toneless, on an even, almost casual pitch.

134

He shifted the glass in his fingers and sipped at its contents. Broadhurst sat looking into the fire. Howard found that he didn't hate the man as he had expected to, any more than he had hated Delgaditio that night in the dungeon of Yuma prison. The three years of domination by a determination that had become almost an obsession had put his mind into a cold groove from which there would be no deviation.

Broadhurst rose and reached for the poker again to stir up the fire. He placed it back, upright against the stone side of the fireplace, and it fell to the hearth with a loud metallic clatter. He set it up again, and Howard let his cold eyes flick toward two doors leading off into rooms. First the glass and now the poker....

Broadhurst said seating himself again, "You told Mary Clay about the girl and she told Nell, who passed it on to Dave. When Dave told me this afternoon that the girl on the stage was your fiancée, I knew the jig was up. In a way, it was a relief. Wells-Fargo and the Pinkerton men don't give up easily, and I was always in fear that the report they turned in on the massacre might have been a smoke screen to cover up what they might suspicion. I'm sorry about the girl, Howard. I really am. She was such a pretty youngster, and I would have like to make an excuse so she'd lay over and take the next stage. But she was the only passenger, and with the stage loaded down with boxes of rifles and about three hundred and fifty pounds of gold coin and silver, I was afraid it would arouse suspicion. So I helped her on and watched them go, knowing what was going to happen. And you're right about the date. Three years next month. What are you going to do now?"

"I'm going to leave the choice up to you," Burt Howard answered. "You can stand trial and hang, or take a ride with me over to a big sand pit at the end of a cul-de-sac. When it rains the water pours off into a deep hole. That's where Luke dragged the cow he had shot when he rustled the calf. That's where I put him, wrapped in a tarp. They're both under fifteen feet of sand. You're right about Dora, Broadhurst. She was a lovely youngster."

"And it was on account of her that you haven't been playing up to Nell Corley, eh?" Broadhurst asked, and actually smiled. Buck, he kept thinking, wake up, you snoring fool!

"It's been three years since she died, and I long ago accepted the fact that she was gone and couldn't be brought back. My relations with Nell are my own business. Bell tired to knife me tonight to get some money I have and fell into a trap I baited. I made him saddle up and he went up to tell Nell good-bye. I heard her scream and went up to the house. He was wrestling with her. He told me the whole setup, how he was working for you, and then went for his gun. But you haven't made a choice yet, Broadhurst. You've got to make one now. I sent word to Tom Wade tonight. He'll be here in the morning. I thought I hated you, but I find that I don't. It's because I can't hate any man, not even men like Lake. Incidentally, he was planning a beautiful double-cross and blackmail game with Dave Bell. They were going to squeeze you dry after I was out of the way."

A rasping voice from the doorway of one of the other rooms said, "That's a lie and don't you move!"

Something like a loud *whoosh* went out of John Broadhurst's lungs as Lake came into the room, a six-shooter in his hand. He was in sock feet, dirty-looking red underwear and still wore his wool shirt, which he apparently slept in. Broadhurst had got up and picked up the gun Burt had not dared to grab for. Lake came over and stood looking down, grinning crookedly. What was in his eyes was all too plain to see.

"Hello, hardcase," he sneered. "It's real funny, come to think of it. We cut your drift fence this evenin' to pull you into a trap, and now danged if you don't walk right into one here on the ranch. How much did you find out, John? I just woke up a minute ago. Want me to work his face over with this gun barrel?"

136

"Not yet," Broadhurst said in his smooth way. "Well, Howard, the shoe is on the other foot. You gave me a choice a moment ago. I'm not giving you one now. With you out of the way, vanished like Luke vanished, I can beat this thing in court for lack of proof. Delgaditio is probably hung by now, and I can deny anything Bell said as the boast of a liar. Wade probably won't be here before morning. That will give us plenty of time. Buck, you go get dressed to ride. Then you can keep him covered while I get on my clothes. The Broadhurst luck is still holding." And he laughed, a hard exultant laugh of relief. His pent up fear had suddenly vanished. It was a laugh of joy, of triumph at the knowledge that the shadow hanging over him for months was gone.

There would be no more of those dreams now.

Lake hurried into the bedroom and soon emerged, having added pants and boots. He sat down with the six-shooter across one knee and poured himself a small drink, yawning while the other man went upstairs.

"I'm going to kill you," he said, grinning. "We'll take you over in an arroyo and I'm going to make you kneel down with yore hands tied back of you and put the gun up close to the back of yore head. But I ain't goin' to shoot right away. I'm goin' to make you wait fer it, not knowing when it's coming. But before I do that, Howard, I'm going to square up for round one that night in the hotel. I'm goin' to stomp in yore face. Hand over that money belt."

"Maybe I haven't got it with me," Howard said.

"You can open yore shirt front and let me take a look or I can slit your scalp open with the barrel of this gun and take it anyhow. Fork over before John gits back. Finders keepers."

Burt unbottoned his shirt front and removed the money belt. He'd forgotten to take it off at the ranch, and he was glad now that he had it. If he could just play on the greed of these two men . . . it was a chance; the only chance he had, he thought.

"Dave Bell said he was supposed to get that as part of his

pay for the job Broadhurst hired him to do. Looks like he didn't come out so well. He didn't get it, he didn't get Nell, and he didn't get me."

Lake was staring at the thick sheaves, golden in the light of the room. He said, "My name ain't Dave Bell, mister," and stuffed the folded belt inside his shirt front.

Broadhurst descended the carpeted stairs presently and came over to the fireplace. "I'll take over, Buck, while you put on your coat. Let's get this done without waking up the rest of the boys."

He picked up the six-shooter, and Lake went back to his room for coat and cap and gloves.

Broadhurst said, "We'll get it over quick so you won't suffer."

"Buck will be happy to oblige," grunted Burt Howard. "He's got more money on him now than he ever saw in one lump."

"Yourn?"

Burt nodded. "It's stuffed inside his shirt front. He says it's all because of this job."

Lake came clomping back into the room, wearing his spurs and a heavy coat and cap over his other clothes. He pulled up and stared as the muzzle of the six-shooter lined his belly. Broadhurst stood with his back to the mantel, and there was too much distance between him and Burt for the latter to do anything about it.

"What's the big idea, John?" the foreman demanded.

"The money. My half of it," the rancher said softly. "Hand over, Buck."

"Like blazes I will! Thet money is—"

"Hand over," Broadhurst interrupted harshly. "I told you—" He paused and swung half around, head cocked. "Listen. That sounds like a trotting horse."

"Maybe one of the boys getting back from town late."

"None of them went in. Buck, take Howard inside the other room. Quick. He's getting down."

138

Under the prod of Lake's gun Howard entered the bedroom. Lake said, "Don't make a false move," and waited, half hidden by the jamb. The front door opened and Tom Wade came in. He had a gun in his hand and he pulled up to look at Broadhurst, who also had a gun in his hand.

"Hello, Tom," the rancher said easily. "Rather late for paying visits to a man with a six-shooter in one hand."

Wade's eyes shot around the room, went back to Broadhurst. He was scared and Howard knew it; but he felt admiration for the man. Wade had conquered his fear and come through.

"Put down the gun, John," he ordered. "You're under arrest. Burt Howard killed your man, Cole Edwards, whose real name happened to be Dave Bell. I know the whole story. Drop that gun!"

"You drop yours," Broadhurst smiled. "You either drop it or we both go down."

Burt's heart almost ceased beating as he saw Wade pause, saw the indecision on his face. He saw the gun start to droop and knew it was all over. Wade, at the last moment, was wilting. Then the hand flashed up level again, and beside Howard, Buck Lake's six-shooter roared. Wade went down, and at the crash of the gun Burt Howard spun and swung with all he had. The blow caught Lake on the jaw and knocked him down, and the gun went into the darkness of the room somewhere. Burt was on him in a flash and pounding wildly at the threshing man in the darkness. Broadhurst ran into the room but could see little except two threshing bodies in a corner. A chair went over with a crash and Broadhurst yelled, "Get him out into the light, Buck, so I can shoot. There'll be the devil to pay now. Hurry before the boys get here."

Burt heard, and he fought savagely as they rolled and twisted. He drove a knee into Lake's groin as they lay threshing and tried to get his fingers into the man's eyes to pop out the eyeballs. Lake was trying to break free, to get up

139

and start his familiar stomping tactics.

Burt's hand was on Lake's big wrist when they both felt the gun at the same time.

But Broadhurst had leaped into the room and was bending down, the gun raised high. Howard lashed out with a free boot and caught him a jackleg blow squarely in the belly that doubled up the man and sent him reeling back against the door jamb. He and Lake had the gun now, were fighting for possession. Burt twisted hard, and then there was a heavy report, muffled because he had the barrel rammed deep into Lake's midriff.

Burt Howard rose and shot the gun out of John Broadhurst's hand.

He said, panting a little, "The offer still goes. I can get you out of here before your men get here from the bunkhouse. What will it be? A ride now or a trial? Your time has run out, Broadhurst."

"I'll stand trial," gasped out Broadhurst, hands on his soft stomach.

He was still hoping; hoping that his men could be brought in at the last moment to regain control of a bad situation. He could hear the sound of running footsteps and knew they were coming. Tom Wade lay on his back on the floor, unmoving, his gun by his hand.

Then from out of the night came running feet and the sound of hard-running horses, and in a matter of minutes it seemed that the place was full of JB punchers and three women, plus Jeb and Shorty and the other NC hands.

Chapter 20

BEDIE WADE, Nell and Mary were down over the sheriff. Bedie was crying softly. Burt went over and knelt beside them.

"He came through at the last moment, Bedie," he said softly. "And if it hadn't been for him it would have been lights out for me. I know how you hate me because I'm the cause of... Holy smokes! He's breathing! Mary, heat some water quick and tear up some bed sheets."

He tore away the front of Wade's shirt. This time the bullet had missed the badly nicked badge. It was in his chest somewhere. While the JB men stood around, scowling and uncertain under the ready guns of Howard's men, they bandaged Tom Wade there on the floor and then carried him over Buck Lake's crumpled body in the doorway and put him to bed.

Burt came back into the living room, and the first thing he saw were the gleaming handcuffs on Broadhurst's wrists. Jeb stood by the mantel, grinning his friendly grin.

"Don't look surprised, boss," he grinned. "Those cuffs ain't Tom's. They're mine."

All of them in the room were staring at him. "You mean that you're an officer, Jeb?" Nell demanded.

"Wells-Fargo, working out of the Pinkerton office in Denver. I ben trailin' this cuss here," indicating Burt Howard, "for a long time now. All the way from Arizona, and of all the slippery cusses I ever saw—"

"Maybe you'd better start in at the beginning," Burt

141

interrupted. "That night you got thrown in jail for being drunk—"

"It began a long time before that, Burt," chuckled Jeb Stuart. "The Wells-Fargo outfit was about to call that Indian massacre of Delgadito's just that, but they're kind of cautious cusses. They got pretty especially curious when you began to backtrack on their men after that stage was burned and the gold taken. They figured that if you smelled a rat then maybe they could smell one. So they put a man on your trail. He shadowed you for a couple of years until you went to Yuma and saw Delgadito. I was just one day behind you and I saw the Indian too. I knew then that Broadhurst was our man. When I slid in town and Mary's father down at the livery told me you were in jail, I faked that drunk to get in and have a talk with you. Wanted to find out how much you knew and warn you not to kill him. But I sorta overdone it. Never was much of a hand at drinking liquor. Just can't take the stuff. That's why I was so sick the next morning. Then I got this chance to go on the ranch were you were the new foreman and I could keep an eye on you while I got concrete evidence Broadhurst was the man. I knew he'd get you if he could, and you'll never know how many days I've trailed you when I was supposed to be working cattle. I was afraid they'd get you with a skyline shot from a rifle. But I should have known you're an Apache country man and wouldn't get caught. Tonight when you lit out I was right on your trail. I was outside the window all the time, listening, and letting Broadhurst put the rope around his neck. About the time the ruckus started, Nell and Bedie and the others boiled in here at a run, having heard the shots as they came across the prairie. So we busted in together. Well," he finished, "I guess that's about all."

"Not quite," Broadhurst put in in a flat voice. "There's still the evidence needed, evidence that a court will demand, and not circumstantial—"

"Mister," grinned Jeb, "we don't need to use circumstantial evidence."

"It's my word against yours, and Delgaditio is dead by now."

"Delgadito is still in Yuma prison," grinned Jeb. "Wells-Fargo made certain he won't be hung until he appears in court to testify it was you who planned that massacre and furnished the guns. This ranch will be taken over by court order, along with the hotel and your other assets, and sold at public acution to recover the eighty thousand in gold you took from the massacre."

"And I'm going to bid in on it," Nell Corley said. Her eyes were upon Burt. "Burt, do you want in as a full pardner, after we chase Kansas and the rest of this gang off the place?"

He said, "We'll talk about it later, Nell," and went into the bedroom. Wade groaned a little and looked up. There was a light in the room now, and the sheriff was fully conscious.

"I've been listening, Burt," he said. "And you were right that night at the dance when you said I was afraid. And I'd have always been afraid if it hadn't been for tonight. I won't be again, and I've got you to thank, if I ever get this slug out of my chest and get well again."

"Bedie won't thank me," he said. "She blames me for it all."

"No, Bedie doesn't blame you at all." her voice said behind him, and he turned. "Bedie is very grateful to you. So you're going to become Nell's pardner?"

"A business pardner."

"Is that all?" she asked, low-voiced.

"That's all, Bedie. I—" He wanted to say it but found that he couldn't. The look in the hazel eyes disturbed him. However, Jeb said it for him. Jeb stood in the doorway, his arm around Mary Clay's waist.

"I've got to report in to the head office at Denver after this mess is over," he grinned. "But Mary and me figured there was no use waiting that long. Why don't we make it a double wedding?"

"Well, why don't we?" Burt Howard agreed.

He went back into the living room. It was almost deserted now. The JB men were gone, Kansas to saddle up and head for the mesa to join the remnants of Dave Bell's horse thief gang. Broadhurst was being prodded upstairs by Shorty and the others to spend the night in bed under vigilant guard. Howard sat down and looked at Nell. He was glad Lake had been carried away.

"I'm glad for your sake and hers, Burt," she said. "It might have been different, but I never struck fire in you. It looks like she did, way down deep."

He sat down in the chair before the fire and a strange contentment such as he had not known in three years stole over him. He felt Bedie's weight on the arm of the chair as she sat down beside him and, since they both knew now, she slid an arm around his shoulders. She did it as naturally as though it were a habit and not the first time. It was Bedie Wade's way.

"Yes," she answered Nell, and tightened the arm around him. "Way down deep, Nell."